# Victoria

*Other works by Knut Hamsun
published by
Farrar, Straus and Giroux*

P A N
*translated by James W. McFarlane*

H U N G E R
*translated by Robert Bly, with introductions by
Mr. Bly and Isaac Bashevis Singer*

M Y S T E R I E S
*forthcoming; translated by Gerry Bothmer*

# Victoria

*a love story by*

## KNUT HAMSUN

*newly translated from the Norwegian*
*by Oliver Stallybrass*

THE NOONDAY PRESS
NEW YORK

# Victoria

# I

The miller's son was thinking as he walked. He was fourteen, big for his age, brown from the sun and the wind, and bursting with ideas.

When he grew up he would work in a match factory. It would be pleasantly dangerous, and he could get sulfur on his fingers so that nobody would dare to shake hands with him. His friends would treat him with great respect because of his ghoulish trade.

He looked out for his birds in the wood. He knew them all, of course, knew where their

3

nests were, understood their cries and answered them with a variety of calls. More than once he had given them pellets of dough kneaded from the flour in his father's mill.

All these trees bordering the path were good friends of his. In the spring he had drained their sap; in the winter he had been almost like a father to them, releasing them from the snow which weighed their branches down. Even up in the abandoned granite quarry no stone was a stranger to him: he had cut letters and symbols on them all, lifted them up and arranged them like a congregation round a priest. All sorts of weird and wonderful things took place in this ancient quarry.

He changed direction and came down to the millpond. The mill was in motion, filling the air with its tremendous booming noise. He often wandered around here, talking aloud to himself. Every drop of spray had its own miniature life history to tell; over by the sluice the water fell sheer, like a brightly colored fabric hung out to dry. In the pond below the fall there were fish; time and again he had stood there with his rod.

When he grew up he would be a diver. That was it: treading his way down from the deck of a ship, down into alien lands, and kingdoms where marvelous great forests swayed their branches and a coral castle lay on the ocean floor. And the princess beckoning to him from a window and saying: Enter!

Then he heard his name being called. His father stood behind him, shouting "Johannes!"

"They've sent for you from the Castle. You're to row the young people over to the island."

He hurried off. A new and wonderful blessing had been granted the miller's son.

The manor house looked like a small castle, a fantastic solitary palace in the green landscape. It was a wooden building, painted white, with numerous bay and dormer windows and a round tower from which a flag flew whenever there were visitors staying. It was known as the Castle. On one side of it was the bay; on the other, the great woods; in the distance you could see a few small cottages.

Johannes met the young people on the pier and helped them into the boat. He knew them already: the Castle children and their friends from the town. Nearly all of them wore high boots for wading; but Victoria, who had on a pair of light dancing shoes and who in any case was no more than ten, had to be carried ashore when they reached the island.

"Shall I carry you?" asked Johannes.

5

"Allow me!" said Otto, a town gentleman of some fifteen summers, and lifted her in his arms.

Johannes stood and watched her being carried well clear of the water and heard her words of thanks. Then Otto said over his shoulder: "Keep an eye on the boat—whatever your name is."

"It's Johannes," answered Victoria. "Yes, he'll keep an eye on the boat."

He was left behind. The others headed for the center of the island with baskets in their hands for collecting birds' eggs. He stood for a while, pondering; he would dearly have liked to go with the others, and they could simply have pulled the boat ashore. Too heavy? It was *not* too heavy. And taking hold of the boat he pulled it up a few inches more.

He heard the group of young people laughing and chattering as they moved away. All right, goodbye for now. But they could perfectly well have taken him with them. He knew of nests that he could have taken them to see, curious concealed holes in the rock harboring birds of prey with tufts on their beaks. Once he had even seen a weasel.

He shoved the boat off and began to row round to the other side of the island. He had covered a considerable distance when a shout

6

hailed him: "Row back! You're frightening the birds."

"I only wanted to show you where the weasel lives . . ." he answered diffidently. He waited for a moment. "And then we could smoke out the adder's nest . . . I've got matches."

No answer. He turned round, rowed back to the landing place, and pulled the boat out of the water.

When he grew up, he would buy an island from the Sultan and forbid all access to it. A gunboat would guard its shores. Your Excellency, the slaves would report, there's a boat aground on the reef, it's breaking up, the young people in it will perish. Let them perish! he replies. Your Excellency, they are shouting for help, we can still save them, and there's a lady in white among them. Save them! he orders in a voice of thunder. Then he sees the Castle children again after many years, and Victoria throws herself at his feet and thanks him for saving her life. There's nothing to thank me for, he replies, I have only done my duty; go freely wherever you wish in my lands. And then he orders the gates of the Castle to be opened, and the party is served with food from golden plates, and three hundred dusky slave girls sing and dance the whole night long. But when the Castle children have to leave, Victoria cannot bear it and falls prostrate, sobbing before him in the dust, because she loves him. Let me stay here, your Excellency, do not reject me, make me one of your slave girls . . .

He began walking rapidly toward the center of the island, trembling with emotion. Yes, yes, he would save the Castle children. Who could tell, perhaps by now they were lost on the island? Perhaps Victoria was stuck fast between two boulders and could not get out? All he had to do was stretch out his arm and set her free.

But when he caught up with them the children looked at him in amazement. Had he abandoned the boat?

"I hold you responsible for the boat," said Otto.

"I could show you where there are raspberries . . ." Johannes faltered.

General silence. Then Victoria said, helpfully: "Could you? Where?"

But the town gentleman quickly recovered himself and said: "We can't be bothered with that now."

Johannes said: "And I know where you can find mussels."

Silence again.

"Are there pearls in them?" asked Otto.

"Just think if there were!" said Victoria.

8

Johannes answered no, he didn't know about that; but the mussels lay far out on the white sand; you needed a boat and you had to dive for them.

So the idea was laughed away and Otto pronounced: "Yes, you look like a diver to me."

Johannes began to breathe hard. "If you like, I could climb that cliff over there and roll a big stone down into the sea," he said.

"What for?"

"Nothing really—just something for you to watch."

But this suggestion too fell flat, and Johannes lapsed into shamefaced silence. Presently he started looking for eggs, far from the others, in another part of the island.

When the whole party was assembled again down by the boat, Johannes had many more eggs than the others. He carried them carefully in his cap.

"How did you manage to find so many?" asked the town gentleman.

"I know where the nests are," answered Johannes happily. "Now I'm going to put them with yours, Victoria."

"Hold it!" Otto shouted. "What's the idea?"

Everyone looked at him. Otto pointed at the cap and said: "How can I be sure that cap's clean?"

9

Johannes said nothing. His happiness evaporated. Presently he began making his way back across the island with the eggs.

"What's the matter with him? Where's he going?" asked Otto impatiently.

"Where are you going, Johannes?" shouted Victoria, running after him.

He stopped and answered quietly: "I'm putting the eggs back in their nests."

They stood for a moment looking at each other.

"And this afternoon I'm going up to the quarry," he added.

No answer.

"I could show you the cave."

"But I'm so frightened," she replied. "You said it was all dark."

Whereupon Johannes, for all his misery, smiled and said boldly: "Yes, but then you'll have me with you."

All his life he had played in the old granite quarry. People had heard him up there, chattering away to himself as he worked; sometimes he had been a priest and conducted divine service.

The place had long since been abandoned, the stones were covered in moss, and almost every trace of drilling and wedging had vanished. But the miller's son had a secret cave that he had cleared and decorated with great artistry, and here he had his abode: the chieftain of the world's most daring robber band.

He rings a silver bell. A diminutive man, a dwarf with a diamond brooch in his cap, comes bounding in—his butler. The dwarf bows before him to the dust. When Princess Victoria comes, show her in! Johannes commands in a loud voice. The dwarf bows down to the dust again and vanishes. Johannes stretches his limbs luxuriously on the soft divan and ponders. This is where he will seat her, offering her sumptuous foods on platters of silver and gold; a blazing bonfire shall illuminate the cave; in its inmost recess, behind the heavy curtain of gold brocade, her couch shall be prepared, and twelve knights shall keep watch . . .

Johannes got up, crawled out of the cave and listened. Down on the path there was a rustling of branches and leaves.

"Victoria!" he shouted.

"Yes," came the reply.

He went to meet her.

"I don't think I dare," she said.

His shoulders swayed as he answered: "I've just been there. That's where I've come from."

They entered the cave. He motioned her to a

11

seat on a stone and said: "That was the stone the giant sat on."

"Oh-h . . . don't go on, don't tell me any more. . . . Weren't you frightened?"

"No."

"Ah, but you told me he only had one eye; so he was only a troll, not a giant."

Johannes considered this point. "He had two eyes, but he was blind in one. He said so himself."

"What else did he say? No, don't tell me!"

"He asked me if I'd like to enter his service."

"You didn't say yes, did you? Good heavens!"

"Well, I didn't say no. Not exactly."

"You must be mad! Do you want to be locked up inside the mountain?"

"I . . . don't know. It's pretty horrible above ground too."

Pause. Then Johannes said: "Ever since those town boys came, you've spent all your time with them."

Another pause.

Johannes continued: "All the same, I'm stronger than any of them when it comes to carrying you or lifting you out of the boat. I'm quite sure I could carry you for a whole hour. Look."

He lifted her up in his arms. She clung to his neck.

"All right, and now you must put me down before you hurt yourself."

He put her down.

She said: "And besides, Otto's strong too. *And* he's fought with grown-up men."

Johannes asked skeptically: "Grown-up men?"

"He has, I tell you. In town."

Pause. Johannes pondered. "Ah, well," he said finally. "Then that's the end of that. I know what I shall do."

"What will you do?"

"I shall sign on with the giant."

"You must be crazy, absolutely crazy!" Victoria screamed.

"I don't care, that's what I'm going to do."

Victoria tried to think of a way out. "Yes, but perhaps he's not coming back any more?"

Johannes replied: "He's coming back."

"Here?" she asked quickly.

"Yes."

Victoria got up and retreated to the mouth of the cave.

"Quick, let's get out of here."

"There's no hurry," said Johannes, who had himself turned pale. "He's not coming till tonight. At the hour of midnight."

Victoria calmed down and was about to sit down again. But Johannes was almost overcome by the atmosphere of horror that he himself had conjured up. The cave had become too dangerous for his liking, and he said: "If you really want to go, there's a stone out there I can show you, with your name on it."

They crept out of the cave and found the stone. Victoria was proud and delighted, Johannes so touched by her reaction he could have cried. He said: "When you look at this stone, you must think of me sometimes while I'm away—spare a kind thought for me."

"All right," Victoria said. "But you'll be coming back, won't you?"

"Goodness knows. No, I don't suppose I shall."

They began to wander homeward. Johannes was close to tears.

"Goodbye then," Victoria said.

"I'll come with you a little farther."

But his feelings were bitterly hurt by her heartlessness in saying goodbye at the earliest possible moment, and his heart swelled with anger.

He stopped abruptly and said, with righteous indignation: "But there's one thing I can tell you, Victoria: you won't find anybody who'll be as kind to you as I've been. That's one thing I *can* tell you."

"But Otto's kind too," she objected.

"All right, take him then."

They walked in silence for a few steps.

"I shall have a splendid time in any case, don't you worry. You don't even know what I'm getting as a reward."

"No, what are you getting?"

"Half the kingdom. That's for a start."

"No, are you really getting that?"

"And I shall have the princess too."

Victoria stopped. "That can't be true surely?"

"That's what he said."

Pause. Then Victoria came out with: "I wonder what she looks like."

"Good heavens, she's more beautiful than anybody in the whole world. Everyone knows that."

Victoria was vanquished. "So you'll take her then?" she asked.

"Certainly," he said, "no doubt about it."

By now Victoria was quite agitated, so he added: "Still, I may come back again some time—take a trip back to the earth."

"But don't bring her with you," she begged. "Why would you want her with you?"

"Oh, I can come on my own if I want."

"Promise?"

"All right, I promise. But why on earth should that worry you? I really can't see why that should worry you."

15

"You've no right to say that, you know," Victoria said. "I'm quite sure she isn't as fond of you as I am."

His young heart was trembling, aglow with rapture. He could have sunk into the ground from joy and bashfulness at her words. He looked anywhere but at her—that was more than he dared. Presently he picked up a twig from the ground, pulled off its bark with his teeth and began hitting his hand with it. Finally he tried to hide his embarrassment by whistling.

"Well, I suppose I'd better be going home," he said.

"Goodbye then," she answered, giving him her hand.

# II

The miller's son left home. He was away for a long time, going to school and learning many things, growing up tall and strong and acquiring a line of down on his upper lip. It was such a long way to the town and the journey to and fro was so expensive that the thrifty miller kept his son there summer and winter for many years, studying all the time.

But now he was a full-grown man of eighteen or twenty or thereabouts.

So one spring afternoon found him stepping

ashore from the steamer. The Castle flag was flying in honor of the son who was coming home for his holidays by the same boat; a carriage was waiting for him at the pier. Johannes took off his cap and bowed to the master and mistress and Victoria. How big and tall Victoria had grown! She made no acknowledgment of his greeting.

He took off his cap a second time and heard her ask her brother: "Tell me, Ditlef, who's that paying his respects?"

And her brother answered: "That's Johannes—Johannes Møller."

She glanced at him again; but by now he was too embarrassed to continue the performance.

Johannes made his way home.

And what a funny little place it was! He had to bend down to get through the door. His parents had brought out drinks in his honor. Powerful emotions seized him: everything was so touching and precious, his father and mother with their gray hair and good hearts, greeting him, holding out their hands to him in turn and bidding him welcome home again.

The very first evening he went on a tour of inspection, visiting the mill, the stone quarry and the fishing place, listening nostalgically to the familiar birds, already at work on their nests in the trees, and making a detour to the great anthill in the wood. The ants were gone, the anthill extinct. He prodded it, but there was no sign of life. As he walked, he noticed how many trees had been felled in the Castle woods.

"Do you recognize the place?" his father asked him jokingly. "Have you found your old thrushes?"

"I don't recognize it entirely. The wood's been thinned."

"It's the master's wood," his father retorted. "It's not for us to count his trees. Anyone can be short of money; and the master's shorter than most."

The days came and went: mild, lovely days filled with the bliss of solitude and with sweet memories from childhood—a renewed call to the earth and the sky, the air and the hills.

He was walking along the road that led to the Castle. He had been stung by a wasp that morning and his upper lip was swollen; if he met anybody he would just bow and walk on. He met nobody. In the Castle grounds he saw a lady, to whom he bowed deeply in passing. It was the mistress of the Castle. He could feel his heart beating as he went past the Castle, just as it had always done. Respect for the great house, with its many windows, and for its severe, distinguished-looking master, was in his blood.

He took the road leading down to the pier.

Suddenly he came upon Ditlef and Victoria. Johannes felt ill at ease: they might think he had been pursuing them. Moreover, he had a swollen lip. He slowed down, uncertain whether to go on. He went on. Long before he reached them he bowed and removed his cap, which he held in his hand as he passed them. They both acknowledged his salutation in silence as they walked slowly by. Victoria looked straight at him; her expression changed slightly.

Johannes continued down to the pier; he was agitated and walked with an air of apprehension. Ah, how tall Victoria had grown, a young woman now and lovelier than ever. Her eyebrows almost came together above her nose, like two delicate lines of velvet. Her deep blue eyes were darker than before.

On his way home he took a path that led through the woods, well outside the Castle grounds. Nobody should say he was dogging the Castle children's footsteps. He came to the top of a hill, found a stone and sat down. The birds were making wild, impassioned music, giving their mating calls, chasing each other, flying with twigs in their beaks. The air was heavy with the sweetish smell of mold, bursting buds and rotting wood.

He had stumbled on Victoria's path; here she came, walking straight toward him from the opposite direction.

A feeling of helpless irritation came over him, he wished he was miles and miles away; this time she was bound to conclude he had been following her. Should he bow to her again? Perhaps he could look the other way; besides, he had this wasp sting.

But when she came near enough he got up and took off his cap. She nodded and smiled.

"Good evening. Welcome home," she said.

Again her lips seemed to tremble slightly; but at once she regained her composure.

He said: "This may seem a little strange; but I didn't know you were here."

"No," she replied, "of course you didn't. It was a whim of mine, I just felt like coming this way. How long are you home for?"

"For the holidays."

He answered with difficulty, she had suddenly become so distant. Why then had she spoken to him?

"Ditlef tells me how splendidly you're do-

21

ing, Johannes. You always do so well in your exams. And he tells me you write poetry. Is that true?"

He squirmed and answered curtly: "Of course. Everybody does."

Now she would soon be on her way, for she said nothing in reply.

"Would you believe it, I was stung by a wasp today," he said, pointing to his mouth. "That's why I look like this."

"You must have been away too long, the wasps don't recognize you."

So it was a matter of indifference to her whether he was disfigured by a wasp or not. Very well. She stood there twirling against her shoulder a red parasol with a gold-inlaid handle, as if that was all she cared about. And yet he had carried her ladyship in his arms on more than one occasion.

"I don't recognize the wasps," he answered. "They used to be my friends."

But this profound remark was lost on her; she made no reply. Still, it really was profound.

"I don't recognize anything here. Even the wood's been cut down."

She winced slightly.

"Perhaps you can't write poetry here then?" she remarked. "Just think if you should write a poem to me one of these days. What am I talk-

22

ing about? You can see how little I know about it."

He looked at the ground in silent indignation. A nice fool of him she was making, talking in this patronizing way and waiting to see the effect. Begging her pardon, he hadn't spent his whole time writing, he'd done more reading than most . . .

"Ah well, I expect we shall meet again. Goodbye for now." He took off his cap and left without replying.

If she only knew that all his poems had been written to her and no one else, every single one, even the one to Night, even the one to the Spirit of the Swamp. But that was something she should never know.

On Sunday Ditlef called and wanted Johannes to go with him to the island. So I'm to be the oarsman again, he thought. He went. Down by the pier a few people were taking a Sunday stroll; otherwise it was very peaceful in the warm sunshine. Suddenly there came the sound of distant music, from over the water and the islands: the mail boat was approaching the pier in a wide arc, and there was a band on board.

Johannes untied the boat and took his place at the oars. He was in a listless, vacillating mood this glorious day, and the music from the

23

ship was weaving before his eyes a tissue of flowers and golden grain.

Why didn't Ditlef come? There he stood on dry land, gazing at the people and the ship as if he had no intention of going any farther. Johannes thought: I'm not sitting here at the oars any longer, I'm getting out. He began turning the boat.

Suddenly a white object streaked across his line of vision and he heard a splash; a pandemonium of despairing cries broke out on the ship and ashore, and a multitude of hands and eyes indicated the spot where the white object had vanished. Simultaneously the music stopped.

In an instant Johannes was there. He acted entirely by instinct, without reflection or conscious decision. He never heard the mother up on deck screaming, "My little girl! My little girl!" He no longer saw any of the faces. Without a moment's delay he leaped from the boat, and dived under.

For a moment he was gone—for a minute; they could see the water seething where he had plunged in and knew he was working away. Cries of distress continued to come from the ship.

Then he bobbed up farther out, some distance from the scene of the accident. Screaming voices and furious pointing fingers told him: "No, it was *here*, it was *here!*"

And he dived under again.

Another agonizing interval, a ceaseless wailing and wringing of hands from a man and woman on deck. Another man, the ship's mate, took off his coat and shoes and leaped overboard. He located the spot where the child had gone under, and now all hopes were pinned on him.

Then Johannes's head reappeared above the surface, even farther out, much farther. He had lost his cap; his head glistened in the sun like a seal's. He was evidently struggling with something, he swam with difficulty, one arm was hampered. A moment later he had got hold of something in his mouth, a great bundle between his teeth; it was the child. Shouts of amazement resounded from land and sea; even the ship's mate must have heard this last outcry, for his head bobbed up and he looked around.

The boat had drifted off, but at last Johannes reached it, got the child aboard, and clambered in after her; all without a moment's hesitation. He was seen to bend over the girl and literally tear the clothes open down her back; then he seized the oars and rowed to the ship like a maniac. As the child was grasped and pulled aboard, triumphant cheers broke out on every side.

"What made you think of looking so far out?" he was asked.

"I know the shoals. And there's a current here. I knew that."

A man forced his way to the side of the ship; he was white as death, with a twisted smile, and eyelashes wet with tears. "Come on board for a moment!" he called down. "I want to thank you. We owe you infinite thanks. Just for a moment."

And the man moved back from the rail, white as death.

The gangway was thrown open and Johannes clambered aboard.

He stayed only a short time. He gave his name and address, a woman embraced him, dripping wet as he was, the pale, distracted man pressed his watch into his hand. He entered a cabin in which two men were bending over the half-drowned child; they said, "She's coming round, her pulse is beating!" Johannes looked at the patient, a young, fair-haired girl in a short dress torn down the back. Then somebody put a hat on his head and he was led out.

He brought the boat to shore, he scarcely knew how, and pulled it out of the water. He heard more cheers and festive music as the steamer headed out again. A great euphoria, cool and sweet, flowed through his being from head to toe; he smiled, his lips moved.

"So our trip's off for today," Ditlef said. He seemed put out.

Victoria was there; she stepped forward and said quickly: "Are you crazy? He must go straight home and change!"

What a tremendous thing to have happened in his nineteenth year!

Johannes set out for home. The music and the loud hurrahs still rang in his ears; powerful feelings urged him on. He went past his home and took the path through the wood and up to the quarry. He looked about for a good sun-baked spot and sat down. Steam rose from his clothes. Wild, restless joy made him get up again and walk around. His heart welled over with happiness. He went down on his knees and, with hot tears in his eyes, thanked God for this day. She had been there, she had heard the people's cheers. Go home and put on dry clothes, she had said.

He sat down and laughed again and again, beside himself with joy. Yes, she had seen him perform this deed, this heroic act, she had followed him with proud eyes as he had brought in the half-drowned girl. Victoria, Victoria! If she knew that he was hers utterly, every second of his life! He would be her servant and slave and sweep a path before her with his shoulders. And he would kiss her delicate shoes and pull her carriage and stock her stove with firewood on cold days, stock her stove with firewood tipped with gold, ah Victoria!

He looked round him. Nobody had heard, he was alone. He held the precious watch in his hand, it ticked, it was going.

Thank you, thank you for this blessed day! He patted the moss on the stones and the twigs on the ground. Victoria had not smiled at him, to be sure; but that was not her way. She had simply stood on the pier, a hint of red flickering over her cheeks. Perhaps she would have liked to have his watch if he had given it to her?

The sun went down and the warmth left the air. He became aware of being wet. Light as a feather, he ran home.

There were summer visitors up at the Castle, a party from town, dancing and music. The flag fluttered from the round tower day and night for a week.

There was hay to be brought in, but the horses were needed by the visiting merrymakers and the hay remained out. And there were great stretches of unmown meadow, but the laborers had been pressed into service as coachmen and oarsmen, and the grass was left to spoil.

And still the music continued in the Yellow Room . . .

During these days the old miller stopped his mill and locked the door. He had learned wisdom: in earlier years the high-spirited town folks had sometimes come in hordes and made merry with his sacks of corn. For the nights were so warm and light, their scope for inventiveness so ample. A certain wealthy court official, a chamberlain, had once in his younger days with his own two hands carried a trough containing an anthill into the mill and left it there. The chamberlain had grown staid with the years, but his son Otto still came to the Castle and amused himself in curious ways. Many stories were told about him . . .

There was a sound of horses' hoofs and voices from the wood. Some of the young people were out riding; the Castle horses were glossy and excited. The horsemen rode up to the miller's door, beat a tattoo on it with their whips, and wanted to ride right in. The door was far too low, but they wanted to ride right in.

"Good evening, good evening," they called. "We've come to pay you a call."

The miller laughed obsequiously at the idea.

Next they dismounted, tethered the horses and started the mill going.

"The hopper's empty!" the miller screamed. "You'll ruin the mill." But his words were lost in the din. "Johannes!" shouted the miller toward the quarry with all the power in his lungs.

Johannes came.

"They're grinding up my millstones," his father cried, pointing.

Johannes walked slowly toward the group. He was terribly pale and the veins stood out on his temples. He recognized Otto, the chamberlain's son, who was wearing the uniform of an officer cadet; and there were two others with him. One of them smiled and called out a greeting to placate him.

Johannes said nothing, gave no sign, but went on walking, making straight for Otto. At that moment he saw two horsewomen coming from the woods; one was Victoria. She was wearing a green riding habit and was mounted on the white Castle mare. She remained in the saddle, watching the scene with questioning eyes.

Johannes changed direction, turned, climbed up on the weir and opened the sluice gates; slowly the noise subsided, the mill stopped.

Otto shouted: "No, let it turn! What are you doing that for? Let the mill turn, do you hear?"

"Was it you who set it going?" Victoria asked.

"That's right," he replied, laughing. "Why's it standing still? Why can't it turn?"

"Because it's empty," Johannes said breathlessly, looking hard at him. "Do you understand? The mill's empty."

"It was empty, you see," echoed Victoria.

"How was I to know that?" Otto said with a laugh. "Why was it empty, I'd like to know. Was there no corn in it?"

"Get back on your horse!" broke in one of the others by way of closing the incident.

They mounted. One of them apologized to Johannes before riding away.

Victoria was the last to go. She went a little way, then turned her horse and came back.

"Please ask your father to excuse this business," she said.

"It would have been more appropriate if the cadet himself had done so," retorted Johannes.

"Of course. Naturally. But . . . he's so full of wild ideas. . . . It's ages since I saw you, Johannes."

He looked up at her, unable to believe his ears. Had she forgotten last Sunday, his great day?

31

He answered: "I saw you Sunday on the pier."

"Yes, of course," she said quickly. "What a stroke of luck that you were able to help the ship's mate drag the bottom. You found the girl, I believe?"

Deeply hurt, he answered briefly: "Yes. We found the girl."

"Or was it," she went on as if a thought had occurred to her, "was it you alone . . . Not that it matters really. Ah well, I do hope you'll mention that other business to your father. Good night."

She nodded, smiled, took up the reins and rode off.

When Victoria was out of sight, Johannes wandered after her into the wood, restless and angry. He found her standing by a tree, alone. She was leaning against the tree and sobbing.

Had she had a fall? Had she hurt herself?

He came up and asked: "Is there anything wrong?"

She took a step toward him, held out her arms, gave him a radiant look. Then she stopped, lowered her arms and said: "No, there's nothing wrong; I got down and let the mare go on ahead. . . . Johannes, you're not to look at me like that. You were standing by the millpond looking at me. What do you want?"

He stammered: "What do I want? I don't understand . . ."

"Why, how broad you are there," she said, suddenly placing her hand over his. "You're so broad there, around the wrist. And you're completely brown from the sun, brown as a berry . . ."

He made a movement to take her hand. But she gathered her riding habit about her and said: "No, nothing's happened to me. I just felt like walking home. Good night."

# III

Johannes returned to the town. And the years and the days went by, a long, exciting time filled with work and dreams, classes and poetry. He was doing well: he had written a poem about "Esther, the Jewish girl who became Queen of Persia" which was published and brought him some money. Another poem, "The Labyrinth of Love," which he put into the mouth of Friar Vendt, made his name well known.

What, then, is love? A wind whispering

among the roses—no, a yellow phosphorescence in the blood. A *danse macabre* in which even the oldest and frailest hearts are obliged to join. It is like the marguerite which opens wide as night draws on, and like the anemone which closes at a breath and dies at a touch.

Such is love.

It can ruin a man, raise him up again, then brand him anew. Such is its fickleness it can favor me today, tomorrow you, tomorrow night a stranger. But such also is its constancy it can hold fast like an inviolable seal, can blaze unquenched until the hour of death. What, then, is the nature of love?

Ah, love is a summer night with stars in the heavens and fragrance on earth. But why does it cause the young man to follow secret paths, the old man to stand on tiptoe in his lonely chamber? Alas, it is love which turns the human heart into a fungus garden, a lush and shameless garden wherein grow mysterious, immodest toadstools.

Does it not cause the monk to creep by night through high-walled gardens and fasten his eye to the windows of sleepers? Does it not possess the nun with foolishness and darken the princess's understanding? It lays low the king's head by the wayside so that his hair sweeps the wayside dust as he whispers lewd words to himself and laughs and sticks out his tongue.

Such is the nature of love.

No, no, it is something different again, like nothing else in the world. It visits the earth on a night in spring when a young man sees two eyes, two eyes. He gazes, he sees. He kisses a mouth, and it feels as though two lights have met in his heart, a sun that flashes at a star. He falls in her arms, and for him the whole world becomes silent and invisible.

Love was God's first word, the first thought that sailed across his mind. He said, Let there be light, and there was love. And every thing that he had made was very good, and nothing thereof did he wish unmade again. And love was creation's source, creation's ruler; but all love's ways are strewn with blossoms and blood, blossoms and blood.

A September day.

This secluded street was his promenade, where he sauntered as freely as in his own room; for he never met anyone, and there were gardens on both sides, and trees with red and yellow leaves.

What was Victoria doing, walking here? What could have brought her this way? He was not mistaken, it was she; perhaps it was she who walked there yesterday evening also, when he looked out of his window.

His heart was beating violently. He had heard that Victoria was in town; but she moved in circles that were closed to the miller's son. He saw nothing of Ditlef either.

He pulled himself together and walked toward the lady. Had she not recognized him? She walked with a serious, pensive air, her head set proudly on her slender neck.

He greeted her.

"Good evening," she answered in a low voice.

She showed no sign of stopping and he walked past in silence, his legs twitching. At the end of the little road he turned as usual. I shall keep my eyes fixed on the sidewalk, he thought, and not look up. Not until he had taken a dozen steps did he look up.

She had stopped at a window.

Should he slink away into the next street? Why was she standing there? The window was a mean one, a small shop window displaying for sale a few bars of red soap, grain barley in a glass jar, a handful of cancelled postage stamps.

Maybe he could take another dozen steps and then turn back.

Then she looked at him and suddenly she

was coming toward him a second time. She walked rapidly, as if she had plucked up courage, and when she spoke there was a catch in her voice. She smiled nervously.

"Good evening. How nice to meet you."

God, how his heart was struggling; it quivered rather than beat. He tried to say something, his lips moved, but no sound came. There was a fragrance from her clothes, from her yellow dress, perhaps from her mouth. At that moment he had no distinct impression of her face; but he recognized her graceful shoulders and saw her long, slender hand on the shaft of her parasol. It was her right hand. There was a ring on it.

For the first few seconds he gave no thought to this, had no sense of disaster. How shapely her hand was!

"I've been in town a whole week," she went on, "but I haven't seen you anywhere. Wait, I did see you once, in the street; somebody said it was you. You've grown so tall!"

He muttered: "I knew you were in town. Are you here for long?"

"A few days. No, not for long. I'm going home again."

"Thank you for letting me talk to you," he said.

Pause.

"Do you know, I seem to have lost my way," she said at last. "I'm staying at the Chamberlain's. Which direction is it?"

"I'll come with you if I may."

They set off together.

"Is Otto home?" he asked by way of conversation.

"Yes, he's home," she replied briefly.

Some men came out of a gate, carrying a piano and blocking their path. Victoria stepped to one side, and in doing so brought her left arm and leg into contact with her escort. Johannes looked at her.

"I beg your pardon," she said.

A thrill of pleasure ran through him at her touch; for a moment he felt her breath on his cheek.

"I see you're wearing a ring," he said. He smiled, assuming an air of indifference. "Perhaps I ought to congratulate you?"

How would she answer? He held his breath and avoided her eyes.

"And you?" she answered. "Haven't you got a ring? No? I'm sure somebody told me . . . We hear so much about you nowadays, in the papers, I mean."

"I've written a few poems," he replied. "But I don't suppose you've seen them."

"Wasn't there a whole book? I seem to . . . ."

"That's true, there was a little book as well."

They had reached a public square. She was in no hurry, even though she was on her way to the Chamberlain's. She sat down on a bench. He stood in front of her.

With a sudden movement she gave him her hand and said: "You sit down too."

And only when he sat down did she release his hand.

Now or never! he thought. Again he tried to strike a playful, indifferent note; he smiled, gazed into space. Good.

"Well, well, so you're engaged and won't even tell me about it. Me, your neighbor back home."

She considered. "That wasn't quite what I wanted to talk to you about today," she said.

Immediately he became serious and said in a low voice: "Of course I knew all along it was no use my . . . I mean, that it wasn't me who . . . I was only the miller's son, and you . . . Of course that's how it is. And I don't even know how I have the courage to sit here with you and hint at such a thing. Because I ought to be standing before you, or kneeling. That would be the proper thing. But somehow . . . And then all these years I've been away have done something to me. It's as if I've gotten more courage. Because now, you see, I know

I'm no longer a child, and I know you couldn't send me to prison even if you wanted to. That's why I have the courage to say this. But you mustn't be angry with me, or I'd rather say nothing."

"No, please go on. Say what you want to say."

"May I? What I want to say? Surely there are things which your ring forbids me to say?"

"No," she answered in a low voice, "it forbids you nothing. Nothing."

"What? Look, what is all this? Why, bless you, Victoria, surely I must be mistaken?" He sprang to his feet and leaned forward, to look right into her face. "Or doesn't the ring mean anything?"

"Sit down again."

He sat down. "Ah, if only you knew how I've thought about you; good God, has there ever been a single other thought in my heart? Of all the people I have ever seen or heard of there was no one in the world but you. The only thought I was capable of was: Victoria is the loveliest and most glorious—and I *know* her! *Miss* Victoria—that's how I've always thought of you. Mind you, I knew perfectly well that nobody could be further from you than I was; but I knew that you existed—and for me that was no small thing—knew that you were there, that you breathed and once in a while perhaps remembered me. Of course you didn't remember me; but many an evening I've sat here in my chair thinking that perhaps once in a while you remembered me. And then, you know, it was as if the gates of heaven were thrown open to me, Miss Victoria, and then I wrote poems to you and spent every øre I had buying flowers for you and went home with them and put them in vases. All my poems are to you, all but a few, and those aren't published. But I don't suppose you've read the published ones either. Now I've started on a major work. God, how thankful I am to you—you fill me to the brim, you are my only source of happiness. Always, at every moment of the day, at night too, something I hear or see reminds me of you. I've written your name on the ceiling, I lie there looking up at it; but the girl who looks after my room can't see it, I've written it in tiny letters to keep it to myself. It never fails to give me joy."

She turned away, undid her bodice and took from it a piece of paper.

"Look!" she said, drawing a deep breath. "I cut it out and kept it. You may as well know, I read it at night. It was Papa who showed it to me first. I went over to the window to read it. 'Where is it? I can't find it,' I said, turning the paper over. But I'd found it and read it already. And I was so happy."

A fragrance from her breast wafted up from the paper; she unfolded it herself and showed it to him, one of his early poems, four short stanzas addressed to her, to the lady on the white horse. It was an ingenuous, fervent outpouring of the heart, a cry that could not be stifled, that rose from the page like stars at twilight.

"Yes," he said, "I wrote that. It's a long, long time since I wrote it, one night when the poplars were rustling away outside my window. No, are you really going to keep it? Thank you! You're keeping it still. Ah!" he exclaimed ecstatically, and his voice dropped down, "to think that you're sitting no farther away than this. I can feel your arm against mine, feel your warmth. Many times when I've been alone, thinking of you, I've shivered with emotion; but now I am warm. The last time I was home, you were lovely then too; but now you're lovelier still. It's your eyes and your eyebrows, your smile—no, I don't know, it's everything, everything about you."

She smiled and gazed at him through halfclosed eyes, gleaming dark blue under long lashes. Her skin glowed warmly. She seemed carried away by joy as she reached toward him with an involuntary movement of the hand.

"Thank you!" she said.

"No, Victoria, don't thank me," he answered. His very soul welled out to her, he wanted to say more, more; confused cries broke from his lips, as though he were intoxicated. "Yes, but Victoria, if you care for me a little . . . I don't know if you do, but say you do even if it's not true. Please! Ah, I promise you, I shall make a name for myself, a great name, a unique name almost. You have no idea what I'm capable of; sometimes when I brood about it I realize I'm one mass of work waiting to be done. Often the feeling pours out of me, during the night I pace up and down my room, I'm so full of visions. There's a man in the next room who can't sleep, he knocks on the wall. At first light he comes to my room, in a fury. That doesn't matter, I don't bother about him; by then you've been in my thoughts so long, it's as if you're there with me. I go to the window and sing, it begins to get light, the poplars are rustling outside. 'Good night!' I say, as the new day starts. It's you I say it to. Now she's asleep, I think, good night and God bless her! Then I go to bed. And so it goes on, night after night. But

I never thought you could be as lovely as you are. Now I shall remember you like this when you've gone—as you are now. I shall remember you so clearly . . ."

"Aren't you coming home?"

"No. I'm not ready. Yes, I'm coming. I'll come now. I'm not ready, but what the hell. Do you still walk in the garden at home sometimes? Do you ever go out in the evening? I could see you, I could say good evening to you perhaps, nothing more. But if you care for me a little, if you can bear me, put up with me, then say . . . Give me that happiness . . . Do you know, there's a palm which flowers only once in its lifetime, though it has a life span of seventy years—the talipot palm. It only flowers once. Now I'm flowering. Yes, I'll earn some money and come home. I'll sell what I've written; I'm writing a major work, you know, and I'll sell it now, first thing tomorrow, as much as I've completed. I'll get quite a bit for it. Would you like me to come home?"

"Yes."

"Thank you, thank you! Forgive me if I'm hoping too much, believing too much, it's so lovely to believe blindly for once. This is the happiest day of my life . . ." .

He took off his hat and put it down beside him.

Victoria looked around. A lady was coming down the street, and farther up a woman with a basket. She became uneasy, took out her watch.

"Must you go now?" he asked. "Say something before you go, let me hear your . . . I love you, now you know. So it will depend on your answer whether I . . . You have me completely in your power. What is your answer?"

Pause.

He lowered his head.

"No, don't tell me!" he implored.

"Not here," she answered. "I'll tell you when we get there."

They began walking.

"I heard you're going to marry the little girl, the girl you saved—what's her name?"

"You mean Camilla?"

"Camilla Seier. I heard you're going to marry her."

"Really, you heard that? She's still a child. I've been to her home, it's a fine big place—a castle like yours; I've been there often. Why, she's still a child."

"She's fifteen. I've met her, we've been together. I was greatly taken by her. She's really charming."

"I'm not going to marry her," he said.

47

"Is that so?"

He looked at her. A shade passed over his face.

"But why are you saying this? Are you trying to divert my attention?"

She walked on with rapid steps and made no answer. They found themselves outside the Chamberlain's. She took his hand and led him in through the gate and up the steps.

"I'm not coming in," he said in some surprise.

She rang the bell, then turned toward him, her bosom heaving.

"I love you," she said. "Do you understand? It's you I love."

With a sudden swift movement she drew him back down three or four steps, threw her arms round him and kissed him. She stood trembling against him.

"It's you I love," she said.

The front door opened. She tore herself away and ran quickly up the steps.

# IV

It was nearly morning; day was beginning to break, a bluish, tremulous September day.

There was a gentle murmuring from the poplars in the garden. A window opened, a man leaned out and hummed. He had no coat on, he looked out on the world like a half-dressed madman who all night long has drunk himself silly with happiness.

All of a sudden he turned from the window and looked toward the door; someone had

49

knocked. He called: "Come in!" A man entered.

"Good morning!" he said to his visitor.

It was an elderly man; he was pale with fury and carried a lamp. For it was still quite dark.

"I propose to ask you once again, Mr. Møller, Mr. Johannes Møller, if you think this sort of thing is reasonable." The man was stuttering with indignation.

"No," answered Johannes, "you're right. I've been writing, it all came so easily, look, I've written all this, I've been lucky tonight. But now I've finished. So I opened the window and sang a little."

"You were bellowing," the man said. "I've never heard anyone sing so loud, do you hear? And it's still the middle of the night."

Johannes reached for his papers on the table and took a handful of sheets, both large and small.

"Look!" he exclaimed. "I tell you, it's never gone so well before. It was like one long flash of lightning. I once saw a lightning flash run along a telegraph wire; God, it looked like a sheet of flame. Well, that's the way my ideas have been flowing tonight. What am I to do? I can't believe you'll go on being angry when you hear the whole story. I sat here writing, you see, I never moved—I remembered about you and sat still. Then a moment came when it slipped my memory, I had to let off steam; and I paced the room once or twice. I was so happy."

"I didn't hear you so much during the night this time," the man said. "But it's unpardonable of you to open the window at this hour and holler like that."

"Yes, yes. You're right, it's unpardonable. But now I've explained to you. I've never had a night like this, you understand. Something happened to me yesterday. I went out in the street and met my joy, my happiness, please listen, I met my star, my happiness. And then, do you know, she kissed me. Her lips were so red and I love her, she kissed me and made me drunk. Has your mouth ever trembled so much that you couldn't speak? I couldn't speak, my heart made my whole body throb. I ran home and fell asleep; I sat here in this chair and slept. Then in the evening I woke up. My soul was dancing up and down inside me from excitement, and I started to write. And what did I write? Here it is! I was in the grip of a strange and glorious flow of ideas, the heavens opened, it was a warm summer day for my soul, an angel proffered wine, I drank it—strong wine, which I drank from a garnet bowl. Did I hear the clock strike? Or see the lamp burn out? God,

51

if only you could understand! I lived the whole thing anew, I walked the same street again with my beloved and everyone turned to look at her. We walked in the park, we met the king, I swept my hat to the ground before him for joy and the king turned to look at her, at my beloved, because she is so tall and beautiful. We went down into the city again and all the schoolchildren turned to look at her, because she is young and wears a light-colored dress. Then we came to a red brick house and went in. I followed her upstairs and wanted to kneel at her feet. Then she threw her arms round me and kissed me. All this happened yesterday evening, as recently as that. If you ask what I've written, I've written a long, continuous ode to joy, to happiness. It was as if happiness lay naked before me with a long, laughing throat and wanted to come to me."

"Look, I really don't wish to continue this conversation," the man said in despondent, irritable tones. "I've spoken to you for the last time."

Johannes stopped him at the door.

"Wait a bit. Oh, you should have seen your face lighting up just then. I saw it when you turned round; it was the lamp, it made a sunspot on your forehead. You became less angry,

I could see that. I opened the window, I know, and I sang too loud. I was the happy brother of all mankind. That's the way it is sometimes. You get carried away. I ought to have remembered you were still asleep . . ."

"The whole town is still asleep."

"Yes, it's early. I should like to make you a present. Will you accept this? It's silver, it was given to me. A little girl whose life I once saved presented it to me. There you are! It holds twenty cigarettes. You won't accept it? I see, you don't smoke, but you should learn. May I come tomorrow and apologize? I should like to do something, ask you to forgive me . . ."

"Good night."

"Good night. I'm going to bed now. I promise you. You won't hear another sound from me. And I'll be more careful from now on."

The man went.

Johannes suddenly opened the door again and added: "That reminds me, I'm leaving. I won't disturb you any more, I'm leaving tomorrow. I forgot to tell you."

But he didn't leave. Several things detained him: things to settle, things to buy, things to pay for; the morning passed, evening came. He whirled around as though demented.

Finally he rang the Chamberlain's door. Was Victoria in?

Victoria was out shopping.

He explained that they came from the same part of the country, Miss Victoria and he, he only wanted to pay his respects if she was in, to take the liberty of paying his respects. He would have liked to give her a message to take home. Never mind.

Next he went into town. He might meet her, catch sight of her, she might be sitting in a carriage. He wandered around until it was evening. Outside the theater he saw her, bowed to her, smiled and bowed, and she acknowledged his greeting. He was about to go up to her, he was a few steps away—when he saw that she was not alone, she was accompanied by Otto, the Chamberlain's son. He was in lieutenant's uniform.

Johannes thought: maybe she'll signal to me now, give me some small sign with her eyes? She hurried into the theater, blushing, head bent as if trying to hide.

Perhaps he could see her in there? He bought a ticket and went in.

He knew the Chamberlain had a box; naturally, rich people like that would have a box. There she sat in all her glory, looking around her. Did she look at him? Never!

At the end of the act he waited for her out in the vestibule. He bowed again; she looked at him in mild surprise and nodded.

"You can get a glass of water over there," Otto said, pointing.

They walked past.

Johannes followed them with his eyes, on which a strange mist had descended. All these people were irritated by him and elbowed him as they passed; he apologized mechanically and continued to stand there. She disappeared from view.

When she came back, he made her a deep bow and said: "Excuse me, miss . . ."

She introduced him, saying: "This is Johannes. Do you recognize him?"

Otto looked at him with narrowed eyes as he muttered an answer.

"I expect you want to know how your people are," she went on, and her face was calm and beautiful. "I don't honestly know, but they're certainly in good health, excellent health. I'll pay them a call."

"Thank you. Are you leaving soon, Miss Victoria?"

"Within the next few days. Good, I'll pay them a call."

She nodded and walked away.

Johannes watched her again till she was out

of sight; then he left the theater. To kill time he embarked on an endless perambulation, a dismal trudging circuit of the streets. By ten o'clock he was standing outside the Chamberlain's house, waiting. The theaters would soon be out and she would come. Perhaps he might open her carriage door and take his hat off, open her carriage door and bow to the ground.

At last, half an hour later, she came. Could he stay here by the gate and remind her again of his existence? He hurried up the street without looking back. He heard the Chamberlain's gates being opened, the carriage driving in, the gates closing again. Then he turned round.

He went on wandering up and down in front of the house for an hour; there was nobody he could be waiting for, he had no errand here. Suddenly the gate opened and Victoria came out into the street. She was hatless, had merely thrown a shawl over her shoulders. She gave him a half-timid, half-embarrassed smile and asked, as an opening gambit: "So you're walking here, deep in thought."

"No," he replied. "Deep in thought? No, I'm just walking here."

"I saw you out here, walking up and down, and I wanted . . . I saw you from my window. I'll have to go straight back."

"Thank you for coming, Victoria. I was in

56

such despair a moment ago, and now it's gone. Excuse me for accosting you at the theater; I'm afraid I've asked for you here at the Chamberlain's too, I wanted to see you and find out what you meant—what was in your mind."

"Well, but surely you know that," she said. "I said quite enough the other day to make it impossible to misunderstand."

"I'm still just as confused about everything."

"Don't let's discuss it any more. I've said enough, I've said far too much, and now I'm hurting you. I love you—I wasn't lying the other day and I'm not lying now; but there are so many things separating us. I'm very fond of you, I love talking with you, more than with anybody else, but . . . I daren't stay here any longer, they can see us from the windows. Johannes, there are so many reasons you don't know about, you mustn't go on asking me what I mean. I've thought about it night and day; I mean what I've said. But it's impossible."

"What's impossible?"

"Everything. Just everything. Please, Johannes, show you've got some pride—don't leave it all to me."

"Indeed I shan't! But I'm beginning to think you made a fool of me the other day. You happened to meet me in the street and you were in a good mood, and so . . ."

She turned and made as if to go.

"Have I done something wrong?" he asked. His face was pale and unrecognizable. "I mean, what have I done to forfeit your . . . ? Have I committed some crime in these last two days and nights?"

"No. It's not that. It's just that I've thought it over—haven't you? It's been impossible all along, you know. I'm fond of you, I respect you . . ."

"And you watch your step."

She looked at him; she found his smile insulting and continued more warmly: "Good God, don't you understand that Papa would forbid it? Why do you force me to say it? You know that yourself. What good would it do? Am I not right?"

Pause.

"Yes," he said.

"Besides," she continued, "there are so many reasons . . . No, you really mustn't follow me to the theater again, you gave me quite a fright. You must never do it again."

"No," he said.

She took his hand.

"Can't you come home for a while? I would look forward to it very much. How warm your hand is; I'm freezing. No, I must go now. Good night."

"Good night," he said.

The street leading up through the town lay cold and gray, like a belt of sand, an endless distance to cross. He came upon a boy selling wilted, faded roses; he called to him, took a rose, gave the boy a tiny gold five-krone piece as largesse, and went on his way. A little later he saw a cluster of children playing near a gateway. A ten-year-old boy sat quietly watching them; he had aged blue eyes with which he followed the game, hollow cheeks, a square chin, and on his head a cloth cap. Or rather, the lining of a cap. This child wore a wig; a scalp disease had disfigured his head for life. Maybe his soul was equally withered.

All this Johannes took in though he had no clear idea which part of the town he was in or where he was going. Then it began to rain; he remained unaware of this and did not put up his umbrella, though he had been carrying it all day.

Eventually he came to a square with some seats, and sat down. The rain grew heavier and heavier; unconsciously he put up his umbrella and remained seated. Presently an invincible drowsiness assailed him, a mist came down on his brain, he closed his eyes and began to nod and doze.

Some time later he was awakened by a

passer-by speaking loudly. He got up and continued on his way. His brain had cleared, he remembered what had happened, every incident, even the boy he had given five kroner to for a rose. He pictured the little man's delight when he discovered this wonderful coin among the small change, realized it wasn't a mere twenty-five-øre piece but a gold five kroner. Go with God!

And maybe the other children had been forced by the rain to go somewhere else and were now playing hopscotch or marbles in the shelter of the gateway. And the disfigured old man of ten sat watching them. Or who knows, maybe he was sitting amusing himself in some way, maybe he had some toy in his little back room, a jumping jack or a humming top. Maybe he had not lost everything in life, there was hope yet in his withered soul.

An elegant, slender lady appeared from nowhere in front of him. He stopped abruptly. No, he didn't know her. She had come out of a side street and was hurrying along, with no umbrella though it was pouring. He caught up with her and looked at her as he went past. How young and elegant she was! She was getting wet, she would catch cold—he didn't dare approach her. Instead he brought down his umbrella so she shouldn't be the only one getting wet. It was after midnight when he arrived home.

A letter was lying on his table, a card, an invitation. The Seiers hoped to have the pleasure of his company tomorrow evening. He would meet people he knew, including—could he guess?—Victoria, the young lady from the Castle. Kind regards.

He fell asleep in his chair. A couple of hours later he woke up, feeling cold. Half awake, half asleep, shivering all over and wearied by his day of misfortune, he sat at the table trying to answer the card, this invitation that he intended to decline.

He wrote his answer and was about to take it down to the letter box. Suddenly it struck him that Victoria had been invited too. Well, well, she'd said nothing about it to him, she was afraid of his going, she had no wish to see him there, among strangers.

He tore his letter to pieces and wrote a new one: thank you, he would come. His hand trembled with suppressed indignation, a strange exultant anger swept over him. Why shouldn't he go? Why should he have to hide? *Basta.*

His violent excitement was now out of control. He ripped off a handful of sheets from his wall calendar, putting himself a week ahead of time. He decided that he was pleased about something, delighted beyond all measure, he must enjoy this moment, light a pipe, sit in his chair and savor it to the fullest. His pipe refused to light, he searched in vain for a knife, a scraper—suddenly he wrenched off a hand from the corner clock to clean his pipe with. The sight of this piece of vandalism filled him with satisfaction, making him laugh inwardly and cast around for further ways of causing havoc.

Time passed. Finally he threw himself on his bed fully dressed in his wet clothes and fell asleep.

When he woke, it was far into day. It was still raining, the street was wet. His head was in turmoil, fragments of his dreams mixed with yesterday's events; he had no fever—on the contrary, his temperature had subsided, a coolness lay before him, like a lake before one who has wandered all night in a stifling forest.

There was a knock, the postman brought a letter. He opened it, glanced at it, read it and understood it only with difficulty. It was from Victoria, a note, a half sheet: she had forgotten to mention that she was going to the Seiers' this evening; she hoped to see him there, she would explain things better, ask him to forget her, to take it like a man. Excuse the wretched paper. Kind regards.

He went into town, ate, went home again, and finally wrote his excuses to the Seiers. He was unable to come this evening, he would look forward to some other occasion, tomorrow evening for example.

He sent the letter by hand.

# V

Autumn came; Victoria had returned home, and the little secluded street was just as before, with its houses and its air of repose. In Johannes's room a lamp burned night after night. It was lit with the stars at dusk and extinguished with the first light of dawn. He was working, struggling, writing his great work.

The weeks and the months went by; he kept to himself and paid no calls, he no longer went to the Seiers'. Often his imagination played crazy tricks on him, obtruding into his book irrelevant conceits which he afterwards had to strike out and throw away. This set him back considerably. A sudden noise in the stillness of the night, a carriage rumbling through the street, could break his train of thought and send him off at a tangent:

"Make way there for the carriage, look out there!"

But why? Why should anyone have to look out for this carriage? It rolled past; by now it might have reached the corner. Perhaps a man is standing there, with no overcoat on, no cap; he stands there bent forward and meets the carriage head on; he will be run over, fatally injured, killed. The man wants to die, for reasons of his own. He no longer buttons his shirt, he has given up tying his shoes in the morning, he goes about disheveled; his chest is bare and hollow; he is about to die. . . . A man is at the point of death, he writes to a friend, a note, a little request. The man dies, leaving this note. It is dated and signed, it has capital letters and small letters, though the writer would die within the hour. Very strange. He has even ended the signature with his usual flourish. And an hour later he is dead. . . . There is another man. He is lying alone in a small room paneled and painted blue. What then? Nothing. In the whole wide world he is the one who

66

must die. He thinks of nothing else; he broods on it until he is exhausted. He can see that it is evening, that the clock on the wall says eight, and he can't think why it doesn't strike. The clock doesn't strike. It is a few minutes past eight and still it ticks but doesn't strike. Poor man, his brain is already going to sleep: the clock *has* struck and he didn't notice. Then he makes a tear in his mother's portrait on the wall—what use is the portrait to him now and why should it remain intact when he is gone? His weary eyes fall on the flower pot on the table and slowly and deliberately he reaches out and pulls the huge flower pot to the ground, where it breaks to smithereens. Why should it stay there, intact? Next he throws his amber cigarette holder out the window. What use is it to him now? There is so obviously no point in leaving it behind. And in a week the man is dead. . . .

Johannes got up and paced up and down. His neighbor in the next room woke up, his snoring ceased, and he was heard to sigh, to groan in anguish. Johannes tiptoed over to the table and sat down again. The wind whistled through the poplars outside his window and set him shivering. The ancient poplars were stripped of their leaves and looked like some unhappy freak of nature; knotted branches scraping against the wall produced a grinding noise like some wooden machine, a cracked stamping mill that never lets up.

He lowered his eyes to his papers and read them through. Hmm, his imagination had led him astray again. He had no business at all with death or a passing carriage. He was writing about a garden, about a green, luxuriant garden near his home, the Castle garden. That was what he was writing about. At this moment it lay lifeless and deep in snow, but he was writing about it all the same and, far from being winter and snow, it is spring and the air is fragrant and the breezes gentle. And it is evening. Below, the water is still and deep, like a leaden sea; the lilacs give off their scent, hedge after hedge is in bud or green leaf, the air is so still that the cooing of the black grouse can be heard across the bay. In one of the garden walks stands Victoria; she is alone, dressed in white, she is twenty. There she stands, taller than the tallest rosebush, gazing over the water, toward the woods, toward the somnolent distant mountains—a white spirit in the midst of the green garden. Footsteps are heard from the road below, she takes a few steps forward, down to the secret pavilion, she leans her elbows on the wall and looks down over it. The man on the road takes off his hat, sweeps it nearly to the ground, and calls a greeting. She nods to him. The man looks around him, there are no spies on the road, he takes a few steps toward the wall. Then she recoils, crying, No, no! and flails at him with her arm. Victoria, he says, what you said once was the eternal truth: I should not have deluded myself, for it is impossible. Yes, she replies: what do you want then? He has come very close to her, only the wall separates them as he says: What do I want? Why, I only want to stay here a minute; it is the last time. I want to come as close as I can to you; now I am not so far away! She is silent. The minute is up. Good night, he says, and again he sweeps his hat almost to the ground. Good night, she answers. And he goes without looking back. . . .

What business had he with death? He crumpled the scribbled sheet and threw it toward the stove, where other scribbled sheets were waiting to burn, mere fleeting whims of an overfertile imagination. And his pen returned to the man down on the road, the wanderer who gives his greeting and then says farewell when his minute is up. And in the garden behind him stands a girl of twenty, dressed in white. She will not have him, and that's that. But he has stood by the wall behind which she lives. So near to her has he once been.

Again the weeks and the months went by, and spring returned. The snow had gone: the distant roar of liberated waters gave the illusion of coming from the sun and the moon. The swallows were back and in the woods outside the town all kinds of leaping beasts and strange-tongued birds had sprung to frenzied life. A fresh, sweet smell wafted up from the earth.

His work had lasted all winter. The poplars, scraping dry branches against the wall day and night, had provided a refrain; now spring had come, the storms were over, and the stamping mill had ground to a halt.

He opened the window and looked out: the street was already hushed though it was not yet midnight, the stars twinkled from a cloudless sky, everything boded a warm, bright day tomorrow. He heard the rumbling noises of the town, mingled with the everlasting roar from afar. Suddenly an engine shrieked, the night train's signal; it sounded like an isolated cockcrow in the peaceful night. Now was the time for work; all through the winter the fluting of this train had served him as a command.

And he closed the window and sat at the table again. He pushed aside the books he had been reading and arranged his papers. He took up his pen.

The great work was almost finished, it only needed a concluding chapter, a farewell message from a ship underway, and already he had this in his mind:

A gentleman sits at a wayside inn, passing through on a long, long journey. His hair and his beard are gray, he is well on in years; but he is still strong and sturdy, and not quite as old as he looks. His hired coach is outside, the horses are resting, the coachman is happy and content, for he has received wine and food from the stranger. When the gentleman signs his name in the log book the landlord knows him, bows low and treats him with great respect. Who lives at the Castle now, the gentleman asks. The Captain, the landlord answers, he is very rich and the lady is kind to everyone. To everyone, the gentleman says to himself with an enigmatic smile, even to me? And he sits down and writes, and when he has finished he reads through what he has written; it is a poem, brooding and dispassionate but full of bitter words. But then he tears the paper to pieces and remains sitting there, tearing the paper into smaller and smaller pieces. There is a knock and a woman dressed in yellow walks in. She lifts her veil, it is the mistress of the Castle—the Lady Victoria in all her majesty. The gentleman rises abruptly, in an instant his dark soul is illumined as if by a beacon. You are so kind to everyone, he says bitterly, you even come to *me*. She makes no answer, just stands there gazing at him, and her face turns dark red. What do you want, he asks as bitterly as before—have you come to remind me of the past? If so, it is for the last time, gracious lady, for now I am leaving forever. Still the young mistress of the Castle makes no answer, but her mouth trembles. He says: Is it not enough that I have acknowledged my folly once? Listen then, I will do so again: my heart's desire was for you, but I was unworthy—does that satisfy you? He continues with mounting vehemence: You rejected me, you took another. I was a peasant, a bumpkin, a barbarian who in my youth strayed into the royal preserve! But then the gentleman slumps to a chair sobbing and begging her: Ah, go! Forgive me and go! All the color has faded from the Lady of the Castle's face. She says, uttering the words very slowly and clearly: I love you; mistake me no longer, it is you I love; farewell! Thus speaks the young mistress of the Castle; then she hides her face in her hands and quickly leaves the room. . . .

He laid down his pen and leaned back. There, full stop, period. There lay the book, pages and pages of writing, nine months' labor. A warm satisfaction rippled through him at the completion of his work. And as he sat there gazing through the window at the first gray light, his head was buzzing and throbbing, his mind was still at work. He was violently excited, his brain resembled a wild, untended garden, with mist rising from the ground.

In some mysterious way he has come to a deep deserted valley, where no living thing can be found. In the distance, alone and abandoned, an organ is playing. He comes nearer, he examines it; the organ is bleeding, blood streams from its side as it plays. Farther on he comes to a marketplace. Everything there is desolate; there are no trees to be seen or sounds to be heard, only a desolate marketplace. But in the sand there are footprints and in the air the last words spoken there still seem to hover, so recently was it abandoned. A strange sensation overcomes him, these words still hovering in the air over the marketplace frighten him, they come closer, they jostle him. He strikes them away and they come again, they are not words, they are old men, a group of old men dancing; he can see them now. Why are they dancing and why are they so totally joyless when they dance? A cold gust blows from this company of old men, they don't see him, they are blind,

73

and when he calls they don't hear him, they are dead. He wanders eastward, toward the sun, he comes to a mountain. A voice calls: are you near a mountain? Yes, he answers, I'm standing near a mountain. Then the voice says: That mountain you are standing near is my foot; I am lying bound in the uttermost part of the earth, come set me free! So he starts out for the uttermost part of the earth. At a bridge he is waylaid by a man collecting shadows, who is made entirely of musk. He is seized by an icy fear at the sight of this man who wants to take his shadow. He spits at him and threatens him with clenched fists, but the man stands motionless, waiting for him. Turn back! cries a voice behind him. He turns and sees a head rolling along the road, showing him the way. The head is a human head and now and again it gives a soundless, mirthless laugh. He follows it. It rolls for days and nights, and he follows it. By the edge of the ocean it slips down in the earth and disappears. He wades out into the ocean and dives down. He finds himself standing in front of a great doorway where he meets a huge barking fish. It has a mane on its back and barks at him like a dog. Behind the fish stands Victoria. He reaches out his hands toward her, she has no clothes on, she laughs at him and a gale blows through her hair. Then

74

he cries out to her, hears his own cry—and wakes.

Johannes got up and went to the window. It was nearly light and in the small mirror on the windowsill he observed that his temples were red. He put out the lamp and by the gray light of day read once more the final page of his book. Then he went to bed.

By late afternoon that same day Johannes had paid the rent, delivered his manuscript and left town. He had gone abroad, no one knew where.

# VI

The great book appeared, a kingdom, a simmering little world of feelings, voices, visions. It was sold, read and placed on people's bookshelves. Several months passed; in the autumn Johannes dashed off another book. What next? His name was instantly on everyone's lips; his success pursued him to the remote spot, far from home, where he had written the book, a book as still and strong as wine:

Gentle reader, this is the story of Didrik and Iselin. Written in a fair season, in the days of small sorrows when all things were easy to bear, written with all the good will in the world for Didrik, whom God smote with love.

Johannes was abroad, no one knew where. And more than a year passed before anyone had news of him.

"I think there's somebody at the door," said the old miller one evening.

He and his wife sat still and listened.

"No, there's no one there," she said after a while. "It's ten o'clock, almost time for bed."

Several minutes passed.

Then there was a loud, resolute knock as if someone had had to pluck up courage first. The miller opened the door. The young lady from the Castle was standing there.

"Don't be afraid, it's only me," she said with a timid smile. She came in; a chair was brought up for her, but she remained standing. She had only a shawl over her head, and light shoes on her feet, though it was not yet spring and the roads were still not dry.

"I only wanted to let you know that the Lieutenant is coming this spring," she said. "The Lieutenant, my fiancé. And he may be shooting woodcock over this way. I just wanted to let you know, so you shouldn't be alarmed."

The miller and his wife looked at the young lady from the Castle in surprise. This was the first time they had ever been warned when guests at the Castle were going shooting in the woods and fields. They thanked her humbly: how thoughtful of her!

Victoria got as far as the door.

"That was all I came for," she said. "I thought: they're old, there'd be no harm in letting them know."

The miller said: "Fancy the young lady thinking of that! And now the young lady has gotten her feet wet."

"No, the road's dry," she said curtly. "I was walking this way in any case. Good night."

She raised the latch and went out. In the doorway she turned. "By the way—Johannes, have you heard from him?"

"No, not a word from him, thank you kindly. Not a word."

"He'll be coming soon, no doubt. I thought maybe you had some news."

"No, not since last spring. Johannes is in foreign parts, they say."

"Ah yes, in foreign parts. He's doing well. He says in one of his books that he's in the days of small sorrows. So he must be doing well."

"Ah, God knows. We're expecting him; but he doesn't write to us, or to anyone. We're just expecting him."

"Maybe he's doing better where he is, since his sorrows are small. Ah well, it's up to him. I only wanted to know if he was coming home this spring. Good night again."

"Good night."

The miller and his wife followed her to the door and watched her set off toward the Castle with her head held high, stepping lightly over the puddles in the sodden lane.

A few days later a letter arrived from Johannes. He was coming home in just over a month from now, when his latest book was finished. Things had been going well for him all this time, another book was nearly ready, his brain had been seething with life. . . .

The miller set out for the Castle. On the way he found a handkerchief marked with Victoria's initials; she must have dropped it the other evening.

The young lady of the Castle was upstairs, but a maid volunteered to take the message—what was the message?

The miller declined to give it. He would prefer to wait.

At last the young lady appeared.

"You wished to speak to me?" she said, opening the door of one of the rooms.

The miller entered the room, returned the handkerchief and said: "And we've had a letter from Johannes."

For an instant her face showed a flicker of happiness. "Thank you so much. Yes, the handkerchief is mine."

"And he's coming home," the miller went on, almost in a whisper.

Her expression froze. "Speak up, miller—who is coming?" she said.

"Johannes."

"Johannes. Well, what about it?"

"Oh, it was . . . We thought I ought to tell you. We talked about it, my wife and I, and she thought so, too. You were asking the other day if he was coming home this spring. Well, he's coming."

"I'm sure you must be pleased," said the young lady of the Castle. "When is he coming?"

"In a month."

"I see. Well, was there anything else?"

"No. We just thought that since you had asked . . . No, there was nothing else. Only what I told you."

The miller had dropped his voice again.

She saw him out. In the passage they met her father and as they passed she said to him in a loud, indifferent voice: "The miller tells me Johannes is coming home. You remember Johannes?"

And the miller went out through the Castle gate, vowing to himself that never, never again would he be such a fool as to listen to his wife when she wanted to get to the bottom of something. And he intended to tell her so.

# VII

The slender mountain ash by the millpond had once caught his eye as a likely fishing rod; now, many years later, it was thicker than his arm. He looked at it in wonder and walked on.

Along the riverbank the impenetrable thicket of bracken still flourished, a perfect jungle through which the cattle had trampled their paths, arched over with interlocking fronds. He fought his way through the thicket as he had done as a child, swimming with his hands and feeling his way with his feet. Insects and crawling things fled before the mighty man.

Up by the granite quarry he found black-thorn, white anemones and violets. He picked a few, their homey smell recalling bygone days. In the distance the hills of the neighboring parish had a bluish tinge and across the bay the cuckoo launched its call.

He sat down; presently he started to hum. Then he heard footsteps lower down the path.

It was evening, the sun was gone, but its warmth still quivered in the air. Over the woods, hills and bay there hung an infinite calm. A woman was coming up toward the quarry. It was Victoria. She was carrying a basket.

Johannes rose, said good evening and made as if to go.

"I didn't want to disturb you," she said. "There were some flowers I wanted to pick."

He made no reply. Nor did it occur to him that she had every conceivable kind of flower in her own garden.

"I brought a basket to put the flowers in," she went on. "But perhaps I shan't find any. We need them for the party, to put on the table. We're having a party."

"Here you'll find anemones and violets," he

84

said. "Higher up there are usually hops. But it may be too early in the year."

"You're paler than last time I saw you," she remarked. "That was over two years ago. You've been away, I hear. I've read your books."

Again he did not answer. It occurred to him that perhaps he could say, "Well, good evening, Miss Victoria," and go. From where he stood it was one step down to the next stone, from there another down to her, and after that he could leave very naturally. She stood right in his path. She was wearing a yellow dress and a red hat, she was mysterious and beautiful; her throat was bare.

"I'm blocking your path," he mumbled and he took a step down. He managed not to betray any emotion.

Now there was only one step between them. She made no effort to move, but simply stood there. They looked each other in the face. Suddenly she blushed crimson, dropped her eyes and moved to one side; her face wore an expression of bewilderment, but she smiled.

He stepped past her, then stopped; her mournful smile smote him, his heart flew out to her, and he said at random: "Well, you must have been in town many times since, I imagine? Since that time? . . . Now I remember where there were always flowers in the old days: on the hillock by your flagstaff."

She turned to look at him and he observed with surprise that her face was pale and tense.

"Will you come that evening?" she said. "Will you come to our party? We're having a party," she continued, and her color began to return. "There are people coming from town. It's quite soon—I'll let you know the details. What do you say?"

He made no answer. It was no party for him, he didn't fit in at the Castle.

"You mustn't say no. You won't be bored, I've thought of that, I've got a surprise for you."

Pause.

"You can't surprise me any more," he said.

She bit her lip; again the despairing smile passed across her face.

"What do you expect me to do?" she said tonelessly.

"I don't expect you to do anything, Miss Victoria. I was sitting here on a stone—I'll go if you like."

"Look, I've been home all day, then I came up here. I could perfectly well have walked along the river, or gone in some other direction, I needn't have come here . . ."

"My dear young lady, the place is yours, not mine."

"I did you an injury once, Johannes, I wanted to make up for it, to make it right. I really have a surprise which I think . . . that is, which I hope you'll be pleased with. I can't say more. But I do want to invite you this time."

"If it can give you any pleasure, then I'll come."

"Will you?"

"Yes, and thank you for your kindness."

When he reached the wood, he turned and looked back. She was sitting; her basket was beside her. He didn't go home but went on pacing up and down the road, filled with a thousand conflicting thoughts. A surprise? She had just said so, a few moments ago, her voice had trembled. A warm, nervous joy awoke in him, his heart beat violently and he felt he was walking on air. And was it a mere coincidence that today she was wearing a yellow dress? He had noticed the hand on which she had once worn a ring—there was no ring there now.

An hour went by. Scents from the woods and meadows swirled round him, seeping into his lungs, into his heart. He sat down, lay back with his hands folded under his head and listened for a long time to the cuckoo's flutelike notes across the bay. Impassioned birdsong quivered in the air.

So it had happened to him once more! When she came up to him in the quarry she had looked like a vagrant butterfly, flitting from stone to stone and coming to light before him. "I didn't want to disturb you," she had said, smiling; her smile was red, her whole face lit up, she scattered stars about her. Her neck had delicate blue veins, and the few freckles under her eyes gave her face a warm hue. She was twenty.

A surprise? What did she intend? Perhaps she would show him his books, bring out those two or three volumes to please him because she had bought them and cut the pages? Please accept this modicum of attention, this consolation prize! Do not despise my humble offering!

He pulled himself violently to his feet. Victoria was coming back; her basket was empty.

"You didn't find any flowers?" he asked absently.

"No, I gave up looking. Or rather, I didn't even begin—I just sat there."

He said: "While I think of it—you don't in the least need to go on thinking you've done me an injury. You have nothing to make up for with any kind of consolation prize."

"No?" she said, taken by surprise. She

thought it over, looking at him and musing. "No? I thought that time . . . I didn't want you to bear me a grudge for what happened."

"It's all right, I don't bear you a grudge."

She thought a little longer. Suddenly she drew herself up. "It's all right then," she said. "I might have known. It couldn't have made that much of an impression. Very well, we won't say any more about it."

"No, indeed we shan't. My impressions are a matter of indifference to you, now as before."

"Goodbye," she said. "Goodbye for now."

"Goodbye," he answered.

They went their separate ways. He stopped and turned. There she went! He stretched out his hands, whispering to himself words of tenderness: I don't bear you a grudge, oh, no; I love you still, love you . . .

"Victoria!" he cried.

She heard him, started and turned round, but continued walking.

Several days passed. Johannes was filled with unease: unable to work, unable to sleep, he spent nearly all his time in the woods. He climbed the great pine-clad hillock where the Castle flagstaff stood; the flag was flying. So was the flag on the round tower of the Castle.

A strange tension held him in its grip. Guests

were expected at the Castle, festivities were afoot. The afternoon was warm and still; the river flowed like a pulse through the torrid landscape. A steamer came gliding into land, leaving a trail of white streaks across the bay. And now four carriages drove out from the Castle yard and down to the pier. The ship tied up; ladies and gentlemen came ashore and took seats in the carriages. A salvo of shots came from the Castle; two men with sporting rifles stood in the round tower, loading and firing, loading and firing. When they had let off twenty-one rounds, the carriages rolled in through the Castle gates and the firing ceased.

Yes, festivities were afoot at the Castle, with flags and salutes to welcome the visitors. In the carriages there were officers in uniform; perhaps Otto, the Lieutenant, was among them.

Johannes descended the hillock and set off for home. He was overtaken and stopped by a man from the Castle. The man had a letter in his cap; he had been sent by Miss Victoria and required an answer.

Johannes read the letter with a beating heart. Victoria had invited him after all, addressing him in cordial terms and begging him to come. This was the occasion she wanted to ask him for. Reply by the messenger.

A wonderful, unexpected happiness was his;

90

the blood mounted to his head and he told the man he would come; yes, thank you, he would come right away.

"That's for you." He handed the messenger an absurdly large tip and ran home to change.

# VIII

For the first time in his life he entered the Castle door and climbed the staircase to the second floor. A buzz of voices reached him from within, his heart thumped, he knocked and went in.

The still youthful hostess came forward, shook his hand and welcomed him warmly. So glad to see him, she remembered him when he was only *so* high; and now he was a great man. . . . She seemed to want to say something

93

more; she held his hand for a long time and looked at him searchingly.

And the master in turn came forward and gave him his hand. As his wife had said, a great man, in more than one sense. A famous man. Very glad . . .

He was introduced to gentlemen and to ladies, to the Chamberlain, who was wearing his decorations, to the Chamberlain's wife, to a neighboring squire, and to Otto, the Lieutenant. Of Victoria there was no sign.

The moments passed. Then Victoria came in, pale, diffident even; she was leading a young girl by the hand. They made a tour of the room, shaking hands with all the guests, saying a few words to each. They stopped in front of Johannes. Victoria smiled and said: "Look, here's Camilla—isn't this a surprise? You know each other."

She stood for a moment looking at them both; then she left the room.

For the first few seconds Johannes stood stunned, rooted to the spot. Isn't that a surprise: Victoria had been kind enough to provide a substitute. Look, you two, go and enjoy one another! Spring is in full bloom, the sun is shining; open the windows if you like, for there is perfume in the garden, even the starlings are making love in the birchtops. Why aren't

94

you talking to each other? Come on, laugh!

"Yes, we know each other," Camilla said ingenuously. "It was here you fished me out of the water that time."

She was young, fair, gay, dressed in pink, not yet seventeen. Johannes clenched his teeth and laughed and joked. Little by little he began to find her cheerful words genuinely refreshing; they talked for a long time, his heartbeat quieted down. She still had from her childhood a charming habit of cocking her head and listening expectantly while he talked. He remembered her well; she had no surprises for him.

Victoria came in again, took the Lieutenant by the elbow, led him over to Johannes and said: "Do you know Otto—my fiancé? I expect you remember him."

The gentlemen remembered each other. They spoke the necessary words, made the necessary bows and parted company. Johannes was left alone with Victoria. He said: "Was that the surprise?"

"Yes," she answered in a hurt, impatient tone. "I did the best I could, I didn't know what else to do. Now don't be unreasonable—thank me instead; I could see you were pleased."

"Thank you, then. Yes, I was pleased."

A feeling of utter despair descended on him;

his face turned white as a sheet. If she had ever done him an injury, he was now richly recompensed and consoled. He was sincerely grateful to her.

"And I see you're wearing your ring today," he added in hollow tones. "Now don't go taking it off again."

Pause.

"No, I'm certainly not taking it off again now," she said.

Their eyes met. His lips trembled, he jerked his head in the direction of the Lieutenant and said, in a hoarse, gruff voice: "You have good taste, Miss Victoria. He's a handsome man. His epaulettes give him a pair of shoulders."

Very calmly she retorted: "No, he's not handsome. But he's well-bred. That counts for something too."

"That was for my benefit. Thank you!" He laughed aloud and added impudently: "And he's got money in his pockets, which counts for still more."

She walked away at once.

He drifted from corner to corner like an outlaw. Camilla spoke to him, asking him questions that he neither heard nor answered. Again she said something; she even touched his arm and asked the question again, with the same lack of success.

"Look, he's thinking!" she exclaimed with a laugh. "He's thinking, he's thinking!"

Victoria heard her and said: "He wants to be alone. He got rid of me too." Then suddenly she came right up to him and said in a loud voice: "I'm sure you're busy thinking up an apology. You don't need to worry about that. On the contrary, I owe you an apology for sending you the invitation so late. It was very inattentive of me. I forgot you till the very last moment, I almost forgot you altogether. But I hope you'll forgive me, because I had so many things to think of."

He stared at her, speechless; even Camilla looked from one to the other with an air of surprise. Victoria stood before them with an expression of satisfaction on her cold, pale face. She had had her revenge.

"That's our young cavaliers for you," she said to Camilla. "We mustn't expect too much of them. There you have my fiancé, sitting there talking about elk-hunting, and here we have the poet, standing around thinking. . . . Say something, poet!"

He started; the veins on his temples stood out.

"Very well. You want me to say something? Very well."

"Oh no, don't exert yourself."

She was on the point of leaving.

"To come straight to the point," he said slowly, smiling though his voice trembled, "not to beat about the bush: have you been in love recently, Miss Victoria?"

For a few seconds there was complete silence; all three could hear their hearts thumping. Camilla put in anxiously: "Victoria's in love with her fiancé, of course. She's just become engaged—didn't you know that?"

The doors to the dining room were thrown open.

Johannes found his place and stood by the chair. The whole table danced before his eyes; he saw a mass of people and heard a babel of voices.

"Yes, that's your place, do sit down," said the hostess kindly. "If only everybody would sit down."

"Excuse me!" said Victoria suddenly from just behind him.

He stepped to one side.

She took his card and moved it several places down, seven places down, next to an old man who had once been the Castle children's tutor and who reputedly drank. She came back with another card and sat down.

He stood and watched the whole performance. The hostess, greatly embarrassed, busied herself with something on the other side of the table and avoided catching his eye.

Shaken and more bewildered than ever, he made his way to the new place; the original one was now occupied by one of Ditlef's friends from town, a young man with diamond studs in his shirt front. On his left sat Victoria, on his right Camilla.

And the dinner began.

The old tutor remembered Johannes as a boy, and a conversation started up between them. The tutor said that he, too, had practiced the art of poetry in his younger days; he still had the manuscripts—perhaps Johannes would read them when he had time. Now he had been summoned to the house on this special day to share in the family's happiness over Victoria's engagement. The master and mistress of the house had planned this surprise for him for the sake of old friendship.

"I haven't read anything of yours," he said. "When I want to read anything, I read myself; I have a drawer full of poems and stories. They're going to be published after my death. After all, I want the public to know who I was. Dear me, we older members of the profession aren't in such a hurry to see everything in print as they are nowadays. Your health!"

99

The meal proceeded. The host rapped on his glass and rose to his feet. His lean, aristocratic face was alive with emotion, and he gave an impression of deep contentment. Johannes inclined his head very low. His glass was empty and no one had filled it for him; he filled it himself to the brim and inclined his head again. Now for it!

The speech, which was long and felicitous, was received with great jubilation; the engagement was announced. A multitude of good wishes for the daughter of the Castle and the Chamberlain's son poured in from every corner of the table.

Johannes emptied his glass.

A few moments later his shattered nerves were restored, his peace of mind returned; the champagne burned in his veins with a low flame. He could hear the Chamberlain speaking in turn, more shouts of "bravo" and "hurrah," and clinking of glasses. Once he glanced in Victoria's direction; she was pale and seemed racked with pain, and didn't look up. Camilla, however, nodded and smiled to him, and he nodded back.

The tutor was chattering away at his side. "It's a splendid thing, a splendid thing, when two people find each other. That is something which never fell to my lot. I was a young student, good prospects, plenty of talent; my father had an excellent name, large house, wealth, ships galore. I might even go so far as to say I had *very* good prospects. She was young, too, and a thoroughbred. Well, I came to her and opened my heart. '*No,*' she answered. Can you understand her? No, she wouldn't have me, she said. Well, I did what I could, got on with my work and took it like a man. Then came my father's lean years, shipwrecks, liabilities—in short, he went bankrupt. Well, what did I do? Took it like a man again. And now she couldn't keep away, the girl I'm talking about. She came back, sought me out in town. What did she want with me, you're going to ask. By this time I was poor, I had a paltry job as a teacher, all my prospects had vanished, my poems put away in a drawer—and now she comes and says yes. Says yes!"

The tutor looked at Johannes and asked: "Can you understand her?"

"So in the end it was you who didn't want her?"

"How on earth *could* I? Stripped, naked and exposed, a job as a teacher, tobacco in my pipe on Sundays only—what are you thinking of? I couldn't do her an injury like that. All I'm saying is: can you understand her?"

"And what became of her afterwards?"

101

"God, you're not answering my question! She married a captain. That was the year after. A captain in the artillery. Your health!"

Johannes said: "I've heard of women who are always looking for objects of sympathy. When things are going well with a man, they hate him and feel superfluous; when things are going badly and his head is bowed, they crow and say: 'Here I am.'"

"But why wouldn't she accept me in my good days? I had the prospects of a young god."

"Because she wanted to wait till you were down in the dust. God knows."

"But I was never down in the dust. Never. I had my pride and I sent her packing. What do you say to that?"

Johannes said nothing.

"Still, you may be right," said the old tutor. "By God and all his angels," he burst out with sudden vehemence, "you're right in what you say. In the end she took an old captain; she nurses him, cuts up his meat for him and rules the roost. A captain in the artillery."

Johannes looked up. Victoria sat with her glass in her hand, staring in his direction. She held her glass high in the air. He felt a tremor run through him and lifted his glass in turn. His hand was shaking.

Then she called to his neighbor and laughed; it was the tutor's name she called.

Johannes put down his glass and managed to smile feebly at no one in particular. Everybody had seen his humiliation.

The old tutor was moved to tears by this friendly attention on the part of his pupil. He quickly emptied his glass.

"And here I am now, an old man," he resumed, "here I am, walking the earth, alone and unknown. That's been my lot in life. Nobody knows what I've got in me; but nobody's ever heard me complain. What's the saying, you know, about the turtledove? Isn't it the turtledove, the famous melancholy creature which, before drinking, stirs up the bright, clear spring water to make it muddy?"

"That I wouldn't know."

"No? I'm sure it is, though. And that's what I do. I didn't get the one I should have had; but for all that, I'm not so hard up for pleasures. Only I stir them up. Always I stir them up. Then the disappointment afterward can't get the better of me. . . . Look at Victoria there. She drank my health just now. I used to be her teacher; now she's getting married, which gives me great pleasure, I feel a truly personal happiness about it, as if she were my own

103

daughter. Now perhaps I shall tutor her children. Yes, there're quite a few pleasures left in life. But what you said about sympathy and women and bowed heads—the more I think about it, the more right you are. God knows, you're . . . Excuse me a moment."

He rose, seized his glass and went over to Victoria. He was already swaying a little on his legs and walking with a heavy stoop.

More speeches were made, the Lieutenant spoke, the neighboring squire raised his glass to the ladies, coupled with the lady of the house. Suddenly the man with the diamond studs got up and mentioned Johannes by name. He had received permission to do this: he wished to salute the young author on behalf of the young. He spoke in the friendliest terms—a well-meaning expression of thanks from his contemporaries, full of appreciation and admiration.

Johannes could hardly believe his own ears. He whispered to the tutor: "Is it me he's addressing?"

The tutor replied: "Yes. He's stolen a march on me. I was going to do it myself; Victoria asked me about it this afternoon."

"*Who* did you say asked you?"

The tutor stared at him. "Nobody," he said.

During the speech all eyes were fixed on Johannes; even the master of the Castle nodded

104

to him, and the Chamberlain's wife put up her pince-nez to observe him. At the end of the speech everyone drank to him.

"You ought to pay him back for that," said the tutor. "He actually stood there and made a speech in your honor. That should have been the privilege of an older member of the profession. I disagreed with him entirely in any case. Entirely."

Johannes looked along the table toward Victoria. It was she who had gotten the man with the diamond studs to speak; why? First she'd approached somebody else about it, earlier in the day she'd already had it in mind; why? Now she sat looking down, a picture of inscrutability.

Suddenly his eyes moisted with a deep and powerful emotion, he could have thrown himself at her feet and thanked her, thanked her. He would do so later, after the meal.

Camilla sat talking first to one neighbor, then to the other, with a bright smile on her face. She was content; her seventeen years had brought her nothing but happiness. She nodded repeatedly at Johannes and signaled for him to stand.

He stood.

He spoke briefly, his voice deep and full of feeling: To this feast with which the house was celebrating a happy event, he too had been invited—a complete outsider, drawn from his obscurity. He wished to thank both the originator of this gracious suggestion and the speaker who had said so many agreeable things about him. Nor could he omit expressing his appreciation of the kindness with which the entire company had listened to his—the outsider's—praises. His only claim to be present on this occasion was his being the son of the Castle's neighbor in the woods . . .

"Hear, hear!" Victoria cried out, her eyes blazing.

Every head turned in her direction; her cheeks were red, and her bosom heaving violently. Johannes broke off. A pained silence ensued.

"Victoria!" her father said in astonishment.

"Go on!" she shouted. "That is your only claim; but go on!" The fire in her eyes died down abruptly, and she smiled helplessly, shaking her head. Then she turned to her father and said: "I only wanted to exaggerate. After all, he's exaggerating himself. I'm sorry, I didn't mean to interrupt . . ."

Johannes listened to this explanation and hit on a way out; his heart was beating audibly. He noticed that Victoria's mother had tears in

her eyes as she looked at her with infinite for-
bearance.

Yes, he said, he had exaggerated; Miss Victoria was right. She had been so gracious as to remind him that he was not only the neighbor's
son but also the Castle children's playmate, and
it was to this circumstance that he owed his
presence here now. He thanked her—what she
had said was true. He belonged to the place;
the Castle woods had once been his entire uni-
verse; beyond, blue in the distance, loomed
adventure and the unknown. But in those days
he would often get a message from Ditlef and
Victoria to join them for some excursion or
game—those were the great moments of his
childhood. Later, when he came to think about
it, he acknowledged that those hours had had a
significance for him that no one could realize,
and if it was true—as had just been said—that
at times his writing *sparkled,* then it was his
memories of that time that had kindled the
spark; it was a reflection of the happiness his
two playmates had bestowed on him in his
childhood. For that reason they could claim a
large share in his achievements. To the general
good wishes on the occasion of the engagement
he therefore wished to add a word of personal
thanks to both the Castle children for those

happy childhood years when neither time nor circumstance had come between them, for that happy, all-too-short summer day . . .

A speech—a regular attempt at a speech. It was not exactly scintillating, but it didn't go too badly either; the company drank, went on eating and began chatting again. Ditlef remarked laconically to his mother: "I never knew it was really me who'd written his books! What?"

But his mother did not laugh. She drank with her children and said: "Thank him, do thank him. It's very understandable; he was alone so much as a child. . . . What are you doing, Victoria?"

"I'm going to send the maid with this spray of lilac to him in thanks. Can't I do that?"

"No," answered the Lieutenant.

After dinner the company scattered about the many rooms, onto the great balcony and even into the garden. Johannes wandered down to the first floor and into the garden room. There were people there already: the squire and another man were smoking and talking in undertones about their host's finances. His property was neglected, overgrown, fences down, trees felled wholesale; by

108

all accounts he even had difficulty paying the surprisingly high insurance on the buildings and their contents.

"How much is it all insured for?"

The squire named the figure, an impressive one.

What was more, they never economized at the Castle, the bills were enormous. Think of the cost of a dinner like this, for example! But now it looked as if the coffers were just about empty, even the lady's famous jewel casket; that was why they needed the son-in-law's money, to restore their former glory.

"How much do you suppose he's worth?"

"Bah, it's beyond reckoning."

Johannes got up and went out into the garden. The lilac was in blossom; the scent of auricula, narcissus, jasmine and lily of the valley broke against him in waves. He found a corner by the wall and sat down on a stone, completely hidden by shrubs. His emotions had exhausted him, he was weary, his intellect clouded; he thought of getting up and going home, but remained seated, dull, listless. Then he heard a murmur of voices on the gravel path; someone was coming; he recognized Victoria's voice. He held his breath and waited a few moments; then through the leaves he caught the glint of the Lieutenant's uniform in the light. The engaged couple were taking a stroll together.

"This doesn't make any kind of sense to me," he was saying. "You sit there listening to him, worrying your head over his precious speech, and then you holler out. What does it all mean?"

She stopped and drew herself to her full height.

"Do you want to know?" she asked.

"Yes."

She was silent.

"It's all the same to me if it means nothing at all," he went on. "In that case you needn't tell me."

She collapsed again.

"No, it doesn't mean anything," she said.

They walked on. The Lieutenant shrugged his epaulettes nervously and said loudly: "He'd better watch his step. Otherwise he may find an officer's hand boxing his ears."

They took the path to the pavilion.

Johannes remained for a while sitting on the stone, in the same state of dull pain. He was losing all interest in everything. The Lieutenant had become suspicious, and his fiancée had immediately started explaining herself. She had said what needed to be said, had put the officer's heart at ease and resumed her walk with him. And the starlings were chattering in the branches above their heads. God grant them a long life. . . . He had made her a speech at dinner and rent his heart in two; it had cost him a great effort to cover over her insolent interruption, and she hadn't even thanked him. She had raised her glass and drunk. Your health, and watch me to see how prettily I drink. . . . For that matter, watch any woman in profile when she drinks. Let her drink from a cup, a glass, anything you care to mention, but watch her in profile. It's a terrifying sight, the act she puts on. She purses up her mouth, dips only the extreme edge in the drink, and gets desperate if during the performance anybody notices her hand. In fact, never look at a woman's hand. She can't stand it, she surrenders. Immediately she snatches her hand away and begins posing it more and more elegantly—to conceal a wrinkle, a malformed finger or a less than perfectly shaped nail. Finally she can't hold out any longer and asks, beside herself: What are you looking at? . . . Once she had kissed him, once upon a time, one summer. It was so long ago, God knows if it was even true. How had it happened, hadn't they been sitting on a bench? They had talked together for a long time, and

111

when they left he had come so close to her that he touched her arm. Outside a front door she had kissed him. I love you! she had said. . . . Now they had walked past, perhaps they were sitting in the pavilion. The Lieutenant would box his ears, he had said. He had heard him quite clearly, he wasn't asleep, but he hadn't got up and stepped forward. An officer's hand, he had said. Well, well, it was a matter of indifference to him. . . .

He got up from the stone and followed them to the pavilion. It was empty. Camilla was standing by the veranda of the house and called to him: Come along in; there was coffee in the garden room. He followed her. The engaged pair were sitting in the garden room, along with several other people. He got his coffee and found himself a seat.

Camilla began talking to him. Her face was so radiant and she looked at him with such innocent eyes that he couldn't resist her; he joined in, answering her questions, laughing. Where had he been? In the garden? Not true at all, she'd looked for him in the garden and not found him. Nonsense, he certainly hadn't been in the garden.

"Was he in the garden, Victoria?" she asked.

"No," Victoria said, "I didn't see him."

The Lieutenant gave his fiancée an angry glance and by way of warning said to the squire in an unnecessarily loud voice: "I believe you invited me to come and shoot some of your woodcock?"

"By all means," answered the squire. "You're welcome."

The Lieutenant looked at Victoria. She said nothing and sat as before, making no attempt to dissuade him from joining the squire's woodcock shoot. His face clouded over more and more, and he stroked his mustache nervously.

Camilla asked Victoria another question.

At this point the Lieutenant rose abruptly and said to the squire: "Good, then I'll come with you this evening, at once."

And with that he left the room.

The squire and a few others followed him.

There was a brief pause.

Suddenly the door opened and the Lieutenant reentered in a state of high agitation.

"Have you forgotten something?" Victoria asked, getting up.

He danced about by the door as if unable to stand still; then he went up to Johannes and knocked him with the hand as though in passing. After that he moved quickly back to the door and continued dancing about.

113

"Look out, man, you jabbed me in the eye," Johannes said with a hollow laugh.

"You're mistaken," answered the Lieutenant. "I gave you a box on the ear. Do you understand? Do you understand?"

Johannes took out his handkerchief, wiped his eye and said: "You can't mean that. You know perfectly well I could fold you in two and put you in my pocket." As he spoke he rose to his feet.

The Lieutenant quickly opened the door and started out. "I meant it!" he shouted over his shoulder. "I meant it, you oaf!" Then he slammed the door shut.

Johannes sat down again.

Victoria was still standing near the middle of the room. She was looking at him and was as white as death.

"Did he hit you?" Camilla asked in utter amazement.

"By accident. He got me in the eye. Have a look."

"Goodness, it's all red, it's bloodshot! No, don't rub it, let me bathe it with water. Your handkerchief's too rough, look, you keep it; I'll use my own. Would you believe it, right in the eye!"

Victoria too held out her handkerchief. She said nothing. Then she walked quite slowly to the glass door, where she stood with her back to the room, looking out. She was tearing her handkerchief into tiny shreds. A few minutes later she opened the door and left the garden room, quietly and without a word.

# IX

Camilla came walking over to the mill, cheerful and uncomplicated. She was alone. She walked straight into the tiny cottage and said, with a little laugh: "Excuse me for not knocking. The stream here makes such a noise that I didn't see any point." She looked round and exclaimed: "What a charming place this is! Charming! Where's Johannes? I'm a friend of Johannes. How's his eye?"

She found a chair and sat down.

Johannes was fetched from the mill. His eye was inflamed and bloodshot.

"I've come of my own accord," said Camilla as they met. "I wanted to come. You must keep bathing your eye in cold water."

"No need for that," he answered. "But, bless you, what have you come here for? Did you want to see the mill? It's good of you to come." He put his arm round his mother's waist and brought her forward. "This is my mother."

They went into the mill. The old miller took off his cap, bowed low and said something; Camilla couldn't hear him but smiled and said at random: "Thank you, thank you. Yes, I'd very much like to see it."

The noise frightened her; she held Johannes's hand and kept glancing up at the two men with great, listening eyes in case they should say something. She looked just like a deaf person. The mill's many wheels and gears filled her with wonder: she laughed, squeezed Johannes's hand in her excitement, and pointed here, there and everywhere. The mill was stopped and started again for her benefit.

For quite a while after leaving the mill Camilla continued to talk absurdly loud, as if the roar still reverberated in her ears.

Johannes saw her back to the Castle.

"Can you imagine his having the nerve to hit you in the eye?" she said. "But then of course he left immediately, he went shooting with the squire. It really was a dreadful thing to have happened. Victoria didn't sleep all night, she told me."

"She'll sleep well tonight then," he said. "When are you thinking of going home?"

"Tomorrow. When are you coming to town?"

"In the autumn. Can I see you this afternoon?"

"Yes, of course!" she cried. "You told me about a cave which you own, do let me see it."

"I'll call for you," he said.

On his way home he sat for a long time on a rock, pondering. A warm, happy thought had occurred to him.

In the afternoon he walked over to the Castle, stopped outside and sent a message in to Camilla. While waiting he caught a glimpse of Victoria at a second-floor window; she peered down at him, turned away and disappeared into the room.

Camilla came out; he took her to the quarry and the cave. He was in an unusually peaceful, happy frame of mind. He found the young girl amusing: her gay, naïve remarks fluttered round him like tiny benedictions. Today the good spirits were close at hand. . . .

"I remember once, Camilla, you gave me a dagger. It had a silver scabbard. I put it away in a box with some other things; there was nothing I could use it for."

"No, there was nothing you could use it for; but what about it?"

"Well, you see, now I've lost it."

"Ah, that was bad luck. But maybe I can get you another one like it somewhere. I'll try."

They were on their way home.

"And do you remember the great big medallion you gave me once? It was gold, enormously thick and heavy, and it had a special frame. And you'd written some kind words on it."

"Yes, I remember."

"When I was abroad last year I gave the medallion away, Camilla."

"You didn't, did you? You mean you gave it away? What ever for?"

"I gave it to a young friend of mine as a keepsake. He was a Russian. He fell on his knees and thanked me."

"Was he as happy as that? Goodness, he must have been deliriously happy, to have fallen on his knees! You shall have a new medallion to keep for yourself."

They had reached the road leading from the mill to the Castle.

Johannes stopped and said: "Here by this thicket something happened to me once. I was out walking one evening, as I often did, and it was fine, summer weather. I lay down behind the thicket, deep in thought. Then two people came walking quietly along the road. The lady stopped. Her companion asked: 'Why do you stop?' But he didn't get any answer, so he asked again: 'Is anything the matter?' 'No,' she answered, 'but you mustn't look at me like that.' 'I was only looking at you,' he said. 'Yes,' she answered, 'I know you love me, of course, but Papa won't allow it, you see; it's impossible.' He murmured: 'Yes, I suppose it's impossible.' Then she said: 'You're so broad there, about the hand; you have such remarkably broad wrists!' And as she spoke she took him by the wrist."

Pause.

"Yes, and what happened next?" Camilla asked.

"I don't know," Johannes said. "Why did she say that about his wrists?"

"They were nice, perhaps. And then he had

a white shirt above them—oh yes, I can easily understand that. Maybe she was fond of him too."

"Camilla!" he said, "if I was very fond of you, and if I waited a few years, I'm only asking . . . In short, I'm not worthy of you—but do you think you might be mine one day, if I asked you next year or in two years?"

Silence.

Camilla was suddenly crimson with confusion, twisting her shapely figure this way and that, clasping her hands. He put his arm round her and asked again: "Do you think you might one day? Be mine?"

"Yes," she said and threw herself into his arms.

Next day he went with her to the pier. He kissed her small hands with their childlike, innocent expression, and was filled with gratitude and joy.

Victoria was not with her.

"Why is there no one with you?"

Camilla told him, with terror in her eyes, that the Castle was plunged in terrible sorrow. A telegram had come that morning, the master of the Castle had turned deathly pale, the old Chamberlain and his wife had cried out in anguish: Otto had been killed while out shooting the evening before.

Johannes gripped Camilla by the arm. "Dead? The Lieutenant?"

"Yes. They're on the way here with the body. It's dreadful."

They walked on, lost in thought; it took the people on the pier and the ship and the shouts of command to arouse them.

Camilla shyly gave him her hand; he kissed it and said: "Well, well, I'm not worthy of you, Camilla, not by any means. But I shall do my best to make you happy if you will be mine."

"I shall be yours. I've wanted it all along, all along."

"I shall follow in a few days," he said. "In a week I shall see you again."

She went on board. He waved to her and went on waving as long as she was in sight. When he turned to go home, Victoria was standing behind him; she, too, held her handkerchief in the air, waving goodbye to Camilla.

"I was just a little too late," she said.

He made no answer. What on earth could he say? Console her for her loss, congratulate her, press her hand? Her voice was completely toneless; a profound distress showed in her face, the mark of some tremendous experience.

People were leaving the pier.

"Your eye is still red," she said, starting to leave. She looked back over her shoulder.

He was standing there still.

All at once she turned round and went up to him. "Otto is dead," she said harshly, her eyes blazing. "You don't say a word, you're so superior. He was a hundred thousand times better than you, do you hear? Do you know how he died? He was shot, the whole of his head was blown to pieces, the whole of his silly little head. He was a hundred thousand . . ."

She burst into sobs and started home with long, despairing strides.

Late that evening there was a knock at the miller's door; Johannes opened the door and looked out; Victoria was standing outside, beckoning to him. He followed her. She seized his hand impetuously and led him up to the road; her hand was icy cold.

"You'd better sit down," he said. "Sit down and rest for a minute; you're all on edge."

They sat down.

She murmured: "What must you think of me—I don't seem able to leave you in peace for a moment!"

"You're very unhappy," he answered. "You must listen to me now and calm down, Victoria. Is there anything I can do to help you?"

"For the love of God, you must forgive me for what I said today!" she implored. "You're right, I'm very unhappy, I've been unhappy for years. I said he was a hundred thousand times better than you—forgive me! He's dead and I was engaged to him, that's all. Do you think it was of my own free will? Johannes, do you see this? It's my engagement ring, I've had it for a long time, a long, long time; now I'm throwing it away—throwing it away!" And she threw the ring into the wood; they both heard it fall. "It was Papa who wanted it. Papa is poor, he has nothing, and Otto was going to come into a fortune one day. 'You must,' Papa told me. 'I won't,' I said. 'Think of your parents,' he said. 'Think of the Castle, the family name, my honor.' 'All right, I'll do it,' I said. 'Give me three years, and I'll do it.' Papa thanked me and waited, Otto waited, they all waited; but I was given the ring right away. After a time I saw nothing could help me. 'Why wait any longer? Go and get my husband,' I said to Papa. 'God bless you,' he said and thanked me again for what I was about to do. So Otto came. I didn't go to meet him on the pier, I stood at my window and saw him drive up. Then I ran to Mamma and fell on my knees at her feet. 'What is it, my child?' she asked. 'I can't do it,' I said. 'I can't marry him; he's here, he's waiting downstairs; but we can insure my life instead and I'll disappear in the bay or the waterfall, it's better for me that way.' Mamma turned deathly pale and wept for me. Papa came. 'There, there, Victoria, my dear,' he said. 'You must come down now and welcome him.' 'I can't, I can't,' I answered, and repeated what I'd said, that he should take pity on me and insure my life. Papa never said a word but sat down on a chair and began to tremble, racking his brain. When I saw that, I said: 'Go and get my husband; I'll take him.' "

Victoria broke off. She was shaking. Johannes took her other hand and warmed it.

"Thanks," she said. "Johannes, please hold my hand tight! Please! Goodness, how warm you are! I'm so grateful to you. But you must forgive what I said on the pier."

"Oh, that's forgotten long ago. Shall I get you a shawl?"

"No, no, thanks. I can't think why I'm shivering when my head's so hot. Johannes, I need to ask your forgiveness for so many things . . ."

"No, no, don't say that. Look, you're calmer now. Sit still."

"You spoke in my honor, you made me a

speech. I didn't know what I was doing from the moment you got up until the moment you sat down again; all I heard was your voice. It was like an organ, and the power it had over me made me frantic. Papa asked me why I'd called out to you and interrupted you; he was very upset about it. But Mamma didn't ask, she knew. I'd told Mamma everything, I'd told her years ago, and two years ago I told her again, when I came back from town. That was the time I met you."

"Don't let us talk about it."

"No, but forgive me, do you hear, be merciful! What in the world am I to do? Papa's home now, he's walking up and down in his study, it's awful for him. Tomorrow is Sunday; he's decided to let the servants have the day off; that's the only decision he's made all day. His face is gray and he never says a word, he's so distressed by his son-in-law's death. I told Mamma I was coming to you. 'You and I must both make the journey into town with the Chamberlain and his wife tomorrow,' she answered. 'I'm going to Johannes,' I repeated. 'Papa can't afford to let all three of us go, he's staying behind himself,' she said and kept on talking about other things. Then I went to the door. Mamma watched me. 'I'm going to him now,' I said for the last time. Mamma followed me to the door and kissed me and said: 'Ah, well, God bless you both!' "

Johannes let go her hands and said: "There, you're warm now."

"Thank you so much, yes, I'm quite warm now. . . . 'God bless you both,' she said. I've told Mamma everything, she's known all along. 'But, dear me, who is it you're in love with, child?' she asked. 'Do you still need to ask?' I said. 'It's Johannes I love, he's the only one I've loved all my life, loved, loved . . .' "

He made a movement. "It's late. Don't you think they'll be getting anxious about you at home?"

"No," she said. "You know it's you I love, Johannes, you must have seen that? I've longed for you all these years, more than anyone can ever understand. I've walked along this road and thought: No, I'll walk through the wood skirting the road; because that was *his* favorite route. So I do the same myself. The day I heard you'd come home I put on a light dress, light yellow; I was sick with suspense and longing, and I was in and out, in and out of every door. 'How radiant you look today!' Mamma said. I kept saying to myself all the time: He's home again! He's glorious and he's home— that's what he is! The next day I couldn't endure it any longer, I put on my light dress again and went up to the quarry to meet you. Do you remember? And I met you, too, but I wasn't picking flowers as I pretended—that wasn't what I came for. You were no longer glad to see me again; but thanks all the same that I met you. That was over two years ago. You had a twig in your hand, and when I came, you were sitting tapping with it; when you'd gone I picked up the twig and hid it and took it home . . ."

"Yes, but Victoria," he said with a tremor in his voice, "you mustn't say such things to me any more."

"No," she answered anxiously and seized his hand. "No, I mustn't. No, I can see you don't like it." She began nervously patting his hand. "No, I can't expect you to. Besides, I've done you so many injuries. Do you think you'll be able to forgive me in time?"

"Yes, of course, completely. It's not that."

"What is it then?"

Pause.

"I'm engaged," he said.

# X

Next day—Sunday—the master of the Castle came in person to the miller and asked him to come soon after noon to drive Lieutenant Otto's body to the steamer. The miller gazed at him uncomprehendingly; the master explained briefly that all his people had been given the day off and had gone to church; none of his staff was at home.

The master had evidently not slept; he looked like death, and was unshaven besides.

He swung his walking-stick in his usual way, however, and held himself erect.

The miller put on his best coat and went. When he had hitched the horses, the master himself helped him bear the body out to the carriage. It was all done in silence, almost in secrecy; no one was there looking on.

The miller drove down to the pier. Behind the carriage came the Chamberlain and his wife, the mistress and Victoria. They were all on foot. Back at the Castle the master could be seen standing alone on the steps, waving farewell; the wind ruffled his gray hair.

The body was brought on board, followed by the mourners. From the ship's railing the mistress called down to the miller and asked him to say goodbye to the master for her; whereupon Victoria made the same request.

Then the ship steamed out. The miller stood for a long time, following it with his eyes. A stiff breeze was blowing and the bay was rough; it was a quarter of an hour before the ship disappeared behind the islands. The miller drove back to the Castle.

He stabled and fed the horses, then went to give his messages to the master. The kitchen door was locked, however. He went round the house and tried to get in by the main entrance; the front door also was locked. It's the dinner hour and the master's having a nap, he thought. But being a punctilious man who liked to fulfill his promises, he went down to the servants' hall, in the hope of meeting someone to whom he could deliver the messages. In the servants' hall there was not a soul to be seen. He went out again, wandered all round, and even tried the maids' room. There was no one there either. The whole place was deserted.

He was just about to leave when he saw a gleam of light in the Castle cellars. He remained where he was. Through the small barred windows he could clearly see a man entering the cellar with a candle in one hand and a red, silk-upholstered chair in the other. It was the master. He had shaved and was dressed as though for a great occasion. Maybe I could knock on the window and give him the message from his wife, thought the miller; but he remained where he was.

The master looked all round, held out the candle and looked all round. He produced a sack that appeared to contain hay or straw and dragged it over by the door. Then he poured some liquid over the sack from a can. Next he took some packing cases, straw and an old flower stand over to the door and sprayed all these in turn; the miller noticed that he took great care not to soil his fingers or his clothes.

He took the little stump of candle, placed it on top of the sack, and packed it carefully round with straw. Then he sat down on the chair.

The miller stared, more and more thunderstruck, at these preparations; his eyes were glued to the cellar window, and a dark suspicion entered his soul. The master sat motionless in the chair, watching the candle burn lower and lower; his hands were folded. The miller saw him flick a speck of dust from the sleeve of his tail coat and fold his hands again.

At this point the old miller shrieked in terror.

The master of the Castle turned his head and looked out the window. Suddenly he sprang to his feet and came to the window, where he stood staring out. In his face was depicted the whole of human suffering. His mouth was grotesquely distorted; he shook his clenched fists at the window in menacing dumb show; finally, making his threats with only one hand now, he backed off across the cellar floor. As he stumbled into the chair, the candle overturned. Instantly a sheet of flame shot up.

The miller screamed and fled. For a few moments he rushed round the yard in senseless, helpless terror. He ran to the cellar window, kicked in the glass, shouted; then he bent down, seized the iron bars in his fists, tugged, buckled them, wrenched them out.

Then he heard a voice from the cellar, a voice without words, a groan as from a dead man already in the ground; twice the terror-stricken miller heard it before he fled from the window, across the yard, down the road and home. Not once did he dare look back.

When he returned with Johannes a few minutes later, the entire Castle, the great old timbered house, was in lurid flames. One or two men from the pier had also come; but there was nothing any of them could do. All was lost.

But the miller's lips were as silent as the grave.

# XI

Asked what love is, some reply: It is only a wind whispering among the roses and dying away. But often it is an inviolable seal that endures for life, endures till death. God has fashioned it of many kinds and seen it endure or perish.

Two mothers were walking along a road talking together. One was dressed in joyful blue because her lover had returned from a journey. The other was dressed in mourning.

She had had three daughters, two dark and one fair, and the fair one had died. That was ten years ago, ten whole years, and still the mother mourned for her.

"How glorious it is today!" cried the mother in blue, exulting and clapping her hands. "I am drunk with the warmth, I am drunk with love, I am filled with happiness. I could tear off all my clothes, here in the road, and stretch out my arms to the sun and send him kisses."

But she in black held her peace, neither smiling nor answering.

"Are you mourning still for your little girl?" asked the one in blue in the innocence of her heart. "Is it not ten years since she died?"

The one in black answered: "Yes. She would have been fifteen now."

Then, to console her, the one in blue said: "But you have other daughters living, you still have two."

The one in black sobbed: "Yes. But neither of them is fair. She who died was so fair."

And the two mothers parted and went their separate ways, each with her love. . . .

But these same two dark daughters had also each her love, and they loved the same man.

He came to the elder and said: "I want to ask your advice, because I love your sister. Yesterday I was unfaithful to her, she surprised me kissing your maid in the passage; she gave a little scream, a whimper, and went past. What am I to do now? I love your sister; speak to her, for heaven's sake, help me!"

And the elder sister turned pale and put her hand to her heart; but she smiled as if in blessing and answered: "I will help you."

Next day he went to the younger sister and threw himself on his knees before her and confessed his love for her.

She looked him up and down and answered: "I fear I cannot spare more than ten kroner, if that is what you mean. But go to my sister, she has more."

And with that she tossed her head and left him.

But when she came to her chamber she threw herself on the floor and wrung her hands for love.

It was winter and cold out of doors, with fog, dust and wind. Johannes was back in town, in his old room, where the poplars rasped against the wooden wall and from whose window he had more than once greeted the dawn. Now the sun was gone.

His work absorbed him completely: large

sheets which he covered with writing and which grew in number as the winter wore on. It was a series of fairy tales from the land of his imagination, an endless, sun-red night.

But his days varied, the good alternating with the bad, and sometimes he would be working at his best when a thought, a pair of eyes, a word from the past would strike him, quenching his inspiration. Then he would get up and begin to pace his room from wall to wall; he had done this so often, he had worn a white path across the floor, and the path grew daily whiter. . . .

Today, as I am unable to work, unable to think, unable to find peace from my memories, I shall try to set down what happened to me one night. Gentle reader, today I have here an altogether dismal day. It is snowing outside, there is almost no one passing in the street, all is sad, and my soul is unspeakably desolate. I have walked for hours, in the street and in my room, and tried to compose myself a little; now it is afternoon and things are no better with me. I, who should be warm, am cold and pale as a burnt-out day. Gentle reader, in this state I shall try to describe a brilliant, thrilling night. For work compels me to calm, and in a few hours I may find myself happy again. . . .

There was a knock at the door and Camilla Seier, his young, secret fiancée, came in. He put down his pen and got up. They smiled and kissed.

"You haven't asked me about the ball," she said at once, throwing herself into a chair. "I danced every single dance. It went on till three o'clock. I danced with Richmond."

"Thank you so much for coming, Camilla. I'm so sadly out of spirits, and you're so cheerful; that will help me—there, and what did you wear at the ball?"

"Red, naturally. Goodness, I don't remember, but I must have talked and laughed like anything. It was simply gorgeous. That's right, I wore red, no sleeves, not even a hint. Richmond's at the Embassy in London."

"I see."

"His parents are English but he was born here. What have you been doing to your eyes? They're all red. Have you been crying?"

"No," he answered, laughing, "but I've been gazing into my fairy tales and there's so much sunshine there. Camilla, if you want to be a really good girl you won't tear that paper up any smaller than you've done already."

"Goodness, what am I thinking of? I'm sorry, Johannes."

"It doesn't matter; it's only some notes. But tell me now: I suppose you had a rose in your hair?"

"Yes, of course—a red rose, almost black. I tell you what, Johannes, we could go to London on our honeymoon. It's not nearly so ghastly as people say, and it's all lies about its being so foggy."

"Who told you that?"

"Richmond. He said so last night, and he knows. You know Richmond, don't you?"

"No, I don't know him. He made me a speech once; he had diamond studs in his shirt front. That's all I remember about him."

"He's perfectly sweet. Fancy, he came up to me and bowed and said: 'Perhaps Miss Seier doesn't remember me . . .' Do you know, I gave him the rose."

"Did you, indeed? What rose?"

"The one I had in my hair. I gave it to him."

"You seem to have been very taken with Richmond."

She reddened and defended herself warmly. "Certainly not, not the least bit. Surely you can like somebody, think well of somebody, without . . . Really, Johannes, you must be mad! I shall never mention his name again."

"Bless your heart, Camilla, I didn't mean
. . . you really mustn't think . . . On the contrary, I should like to thank him for entertain-
ing you."

"Yes, indeed, you must certainly do that—
just you dare! For my part I shan't say another
word to him as long as I live."

Pause.

"Well, well, let's leave it at that," he said.
"Are you going already?"

"Yes, I can't stay any longer. How far have
you got with your work now? Mamma was asking about it. Imagine, I hadn't seen Victoria for
weeks and just now I've met her."

"Just now?"

"On my way here. She smiled. But heavens,
how her looks have faded! Listen, aren't you
coming to see us soon?"

"Yes, soon," he answered, jumping up. A
flush had spread across his face. "In the next
few days, maybe. I have to write something
first, something I've just thought of, a conclu-
sion to my fairy tales. I'm going to write something, I tell you! Imagine the earth seen from
above, like a magnificent rare papal robe. In its
folds there are people walking about; they're
in pairs, it's evening and peaceful, the hour of
love. I'm calling it *God's Family*. I think it's
going to be powerful; I've had this vision so

often, and every time it's as if my breast is about to burst, and I could embrace the whole earth. There are people and beasts and birds, and all of them are having their hour of love, Camilla. A wave of delight is gathering, eyes grow passionate, bosoms heave. Then a delicate blush rises from the earth, a blush of modesty from all the naked hearts, and the night takes on a rose-red tint. But far off in the background lie the mighty, sleeping mountains; they have seen and heard nothing. And in the morning God casts his warm sun over everything. *God's Family*, I'm calling it."

"I see."

"Yes. And then when I've finished it I'll come. Thank you so much for this visit, Camilla. And you mustn't think any more about what I said. I didn't mean any harm by it."

"I'm not thinking about it at all. But I shall never mention his name again. I shall certainly never do that."

Next morning Camilla came again. She was pale and unusually agitated.

"What's wrong?" he asked.

"Wrong? Nothing," she said hastily. "It's you I'm fond of. You really mustn't think that there's anything wrong and that I'm not fond of you. No, I'll tell you what I've been thinking: we won't go to London. Why should we go there? I don't suppose he knew what he was talking about, that man, there's more fog there than he thinks. You're looking at me, why are you doing that? I never mentioned his name. What a liar! He told me a pack of lies; we won't go to London."

He looked at her attentively.

"No, we won't go to London," he said in a thoughtful voice.

"You agree? All right, we won't go then. Have you written that thing about the family? Goodness, how I want to hear about it! You really must finish it soon and come and see us, Johannes. The hour of love, isn't that right? And a gorgeous papal robe with folds, and a rose-red night—goodness, how well I remember what you told me about it! I haven't been here so often lately; but now I'm going to come every day and see if you're finished."

"I shall soon be finished," he said, still looking at her.

"Today I took your books and put them in my own room. I want to read them all again. It won't tire me in the slightest, I'm looking forward to it. Look, Johannes, I wish you'd be very kind and see me home; I'm not sure if it's quite safe for me all the way home. I'm not sure. Maybe there's somebody waiting for me just outside, walking up and down waiting, perhaps. I almost think there is . . ." Suddenly she burst into tears and stammered. "I called him a liar; I didn't mean to. It hurts me to think I said that. He hasn't told me lies; on the contrary, he was . . . We're having guests on Tuesday but he's not coming, but you're coming, I tell you. Promise? Still, I didn't mean to speak ill of him. I don't know what you must think of me . . ."

He said: "I'm beginning to understand you."

She flung her arms round his neck and buried her head in his breast, trembling and deeply disturbed.

"Yes, but I'm fond of you too," she burst out. "You mustn't think I'm not. I don't only love him, it's not as bad as that. When you asked me last year I was so happy; but now he has come. I don't understand it. Is it so terrible of me, Johannes? Perhaps I do love him just a tiny bit more than you; I can't help it, it's something that's happened to me. Goodness, I haven't slept for nights since I saw him, and I love him more and more. What am I to do? You must tell me, you're so much older. He came here with me now, he's standing out there waiting to see me home again, and maybe he's cold by now. Do you despise me, Johannes? I haven't kissed him, really I haven't, you must believe me, I've only given him my rose. Why don't you an-

146

swer, Johannes? You must tell me what to do, because I can't bear it any longer."

Johannes sat quite still and listened to her. He said: "I have nothing to say."

"Thank you, thank you, *dear* Johannes, you're so kind, not being furious with me," she said, drying her tears. "But you mustn't think I'm not fond of you too. Goodness, I'm going to come and see you much more often and do my best to please you. It's just that it's him I'm most fond of. I didn't want it to happen. It's not my fault."

He got up without a word, put on his hat and said: "Shall we go?"

They went down the stairs.

Outside they found Richmond. He was a dark-haired young man whose brown eyes sparkled with youth and life. The frost had colored his cheeks red.

"Are you cold?" asked Camilla as she flew to him. Her voice trembled with emotion.

Suddenly she hurried back to Johannes, put her arm through his and said: "Excuse me for not asking if *you* were cold. You didn't put your overcoat on; shall I go up for it? No? Well, button your coat at least."

He buttoned his coat.

Johannes offered Richmond his hand. He was in a curiously distant mood, as if what was happening didn't really concern him. He smiled uncertainly and murmured: "Glad to see you again."

Richmond showed no trace of guilt or dissimulation. As he took Johannes's hand and removed his hat, his face was all joyous recognition.

"I've just seen one of your books in a bookshop window in London," he said. "A translation. It was very nice seeing it there, like a greeting from home."

Camilla walked between them, looking up at each of them in turn. Finally she said: "So you're coming on Tuesday then, Johannes— you must excuse me, my mind keeps running on my own affairs," she added with a laugh. But the next moment she turned remorsefully to Richmond and invited him too. They were all people he knew, Victoria and her mother were invited too, and ten or twelve others, no more.

Suddenly Johannes stopped and said: "Well, I may just as well turn back, really."

"See you on Tuesday," Camilla replied.

Richmond grasped his hand and shook it with genuine friendliness.

And the two young people went on their way, alone and happy.

# XII

The mother in blue was in the most terrible suspense: every moment she expected a signal from the garden, but the coast was not clear; no one could get by as long as her husband refused to leave the house. Ugh, that husband, that forty-year-old, balding husband! What ugly thought was in his mind to make him so pale this evening and keep him sitting there in his chair, immovable, inexorable, staring at his newspaper?

149

Not a moment's peace did she have; now the clock struck eleven. Her children had long since gone to bed; but her husband made no move. What if the signal sounded, the door was opened with the darling little key—and the two men met face to face, eye to eye? She dared not complete the thought.

She went into the darkest corner of the room, wrung her hands, and at last said boldly: "It's eleven o'clock. If you're going to the club at all, you must go now."

He got up at once, paler than ever, and left the room and the house.

Once outside the garden, he stopped and listened: there was a whistle, a little signal. Steps were heard on the gravel, a key was inserted in the latch and turned . . . and, shortly after, two shadows appeared on the living-room curtain.

And he knew from of old the signal, the steps and the two shadows on the curtain; they were all familiar to him.

He went to the club. It was open, there were lights in the windows; but he did not go in. For half an hour he wandered around in the streets and in front of his garden, an endless half hour. Let me wait another quarter of an hour, he thought; and he did. Finally he went into

150

the garden and up the steps and rang his own front door.

The maid came and unlocked it, put her head round the corner and said: "Madam has long since . . ." Then she saw who it was and stopped.

"Just so, gone to bed," he said. "Will you tell the mistress that her husband has come home!"

The maid went. She knocked at her mistress's room and gave the message through the closed door. "I was to say that the master has come home."

From within, the mistress asked: "What did you say—that the master has come home? Who told you to say so?"

"The master himself. He's standing outside."

Confused sounds of lamentation came from the mistress's room, earnest whispering, a door opening and closing. Then all was quiet.

And in came the master. His wife met him with death in her heart.

"The club was closed," he said, moved at once to pity and compassion. "I sent a message so as not to alarm you."

She collapsed in a chair, reassured, liberated, saved. In this access of joy her good heart overflowed with concern for her husband's health. "You're so pale. Are you all right, my dear?"

"I'm not cold," he answered.

"But has anything happened to you? Your face is so strangely distorted."

"No, I'm smiling," he said. "This is going to be my way of smiling. I want this grimace to be my hallmark."

She heard these clipped, hoarse words without grasping their sense, without understanding a word. What could he mean by them?

But suddenly he threw his arms round her, in an ironlike grip of terrifying strength, and whispered in her ear: "What do you say, shall we put horns on him . . . on the fellow who left . . . shall we put horns on him?"

She screamed and called for the maid. He let go of her with a dry, noiseless laugh, opening his mouth like a chasm and slapping his thighs.

In the morning his wife's good heart again got the upper hand and she said to her husband: "You had a very strange attack last night; it's over now, but you're still pale today."

"Yes," he answered, "it's a strain being witty at my age. I'm giving it up."

However, after describing many kinds of love, Friar Vendt tells of yet another kind, of which he says:

What rapture there is in one special kind of love!

The young lord and lady had just come home; their long honeymoon was over, and they began to settle down.

A shooting star fell over their roof.

In the summer the young couple went for walks together, they never left each other's side. They picked flowers, yellow, red and blue flowers which they gave to each other, they saw the grass stirring in the breeze and heard the birds singing in the woods; and every word they spoke was a caress. In the winter they drove with bells on their horses, the sky was blue, and high above them the stars raced in their eternal courses.

In this way many, many years went by. The young couple had three children and their hearts were as loving as on the first day, in the hour of the first kiss.

But then came the proud lord's sickness, the sickness that chained him so long to his bed, that put his wife's patience to so hard a test. The day he was well enough to rise from his bed he did not recognize himself; the sickness had disfigured him and taken his hair.

He suffered and brooded over it. Then one morning he said: "Now I suppose you cannot love me any more."

But his wife blushed, threw her arms round him, kissed him as passionately as in the spring of their youth, and said: "Ah, but I love you—love you forever. I shall never forget it was I and no one else whom you chose and made so happy."

And she went into her chamber and cut off all her golden hair in order to be like her husband whom she loved.

And again many, many years went by; the young couple became old and their children grew up. They shared every happiness as before; in the summer they still walked in the fields and saw the grass waving, and in the winter they wrapped themselves in their furs and drove out under the starry sky. And their hearts remained warm and glad, as if from some marvelous wine.

Then the wife became paralyzed. Unable to walk, she spent much of her time in a wheelchair, which her husband himself wheeled about. But she suffered inexpressibly over her misfortune and her face had deep lines of sorrow.

One day she said: "Now I would gladly die. I am so crippled and hideous, and your face is so beautiful, you cannot kiss me any more or love me as of old."

But her husband embraced her, flushed with emotion, and said: "Ah, but I love you more, more than my life, my dearest—love you as on the first day, in the first hour, when you gave me the rose. Do you remember? You offered me the rose and looked at me with your beautiful eyes; the rose had the same scent as you, you blushed like the rose, and all my senses were intoxicated. But now I love you even more, you are more beautiful than in your youth, and I thank you and bless you in my heart for every day that you have been mine."

The husband went into his chamber and threw acid in his face to disfigure it. Then he said to his wife: "I have had the misfortune to spill acid on my face; my cheeks are covered with burns; and now, I suppose, you cannot love me any more?"

"Ah, my bridegroom, my beloved!" faltered the old woman, kissing his hands. "You are more beautiful than any man on earth; to this day your voice sets my heart aglow, and I shall love you until I die."

# XIII

Johannes met Camilla in the street; she was with her mother, her father and young Richmond; they stopped their carriage and spoke to him in friendly terms.

Camilla gripped his arm and said: "You never came to our party. We had great fun, you know; we waited for you right to the end, but you never came."

"I was prevented," he answered.

"Excuse my not having been up to see you since," she went on. "I'm coming one of these

157

days, quite definitely, when Richmond's gone. What fun we had! Victoria was taken sick, she was driven home—had you heard? I shall go and see her soon. I expect she's much better—completely recovered, perhaps. I've given Richmond a medallion, almost the same as yours. Listen, Johannes, you must promise me to look after your fire; when you're writing you forget everything, your room gets icy cold. If that should happen, you must ring for the girl."

"All right, I'll ring for the girl," he said.

Mrs. Seier spoke to him also, asking him about his work, the piece about God's family; how was it going? She was impatient to see his next piece.

Johannes answered appropriately, made a deep bow and watched the carriage drive off. How little it all concerned him, this carriage, these people, this chatter! A cold, empty feeling caught up with him and stayed with him all the way home. Outside his door a man was pacing up and down: an old acquaintance, the former tutor at the Castle.

Johannes greeted him.

He was wearing a long, warm overcoat that had been carefully brushed, and his manner was brisk and resolute.

"You see here your friend and colleague," he said. "Give me your hand, young man. God has guided my steps in marvelous ways since our last meeting: I am married, I have a home, a little garden, a wife. Miracles still happen. Have you any comment to make on that last remark?"

Johannes looked at him in bewilderment.

"Carried unanimously, then. Yes, you see, I was coaching her son. She has a son, a young hopeful, from her first marriage; she's been married before, of course, she was a widow. In short, I've married a widow. You may object that the silver spoon I was born with seems to have dropped out of my mouth; still, there it is; I've married a widow. The young hopeful she already had. I'd go there, you see, and I'd look at the garden and the widow, and I'd rack my brains about it all. Then suddenly I had the answer, I said to myself: Well, what if it isn't the silver spoon I was born with, and all that? I'll do it just the same, I'll take the plunge, for most likely it's written in the book of fate. So you see, that's how it happened."

"Congratulations!" said Johannes.

"Stop! Not another word! I know what you're going to say. What about *her*, you're going to say, what about the first one, you're going to say, have you forgotten the eternal love of your youth? *That's* what you're going to say. Then may I ask you in turn, my most highly honored friend, what became of my first, only and eternal love? Married a captain in the artillery, didn't she? Moreover, let me ask you another little question: have you ever in all your days known a case of a man getting the one he should have got? I haven't. There's a legend about a man whose prayers God granted, so that he was given his first and only love. But that was all the joy he got out of it. Why, you're going to ask again, and if you wait I'll tell you: for the simple reason that she died immediately after—*immediately* after, do you hear, ha-ha-ha, instantly. It's always the same story. Naturally one doesn't get the woman one should have had; but if by some damned freak of reason and justice it ever does happen, then of course she dies immediately after. There's always some double-dealing. So then the man has to find himself another love, whatever's available, and there's no need for him to die of the change. I tell you, Nature has ordained these things so wisely that he manages excellently. Just look at me."

Johannes said: "I can see you've done well."

"Excellently. Feel this coat! Use your eyes and your ears! Has a sea of bitter sorrows submerged me? I have clothes, shoes, house and home, a bedfellow, children—the young hopeful, at all events. What was I going to say? Oh

160

yes, and as for my poetry—I'll answer that question right off. My dear young colleague, I am older than you, and it may be that I am slightly better endowed by Nature. I have a drawer full of poetry. It's going to be published after my death. In that case you'll get no satisfaction from it, you're going to object. Wrong again: what I'm doing in the interval is delighting my household with it. In the evening, when the lamp is lit, I unlock the drawer, take out my poems and read them aloud to my wife and the young hopeful. One is forty, the other twelve—and they're both fascinated. If you'll look in on us one evening, you'll get a bite of food and a drop of toddy. That's an invitation. God preserve you from death."

He gave Johannes his hand. Suddenly he asked: "Have you heard about Victoria?"

"Victoria? No. Or rather, I heard about her a few minutes ago. . . ."

"Haven't you seen her declining, getting grayer and grayer under the eyes?"

"I haven't seen her since I was home in the spring. Is she unwell still?"

With comical ferociousness and a stamp of his foot the tutor replied: "Yes!"

"I heard just now . . . No, I certainly haven't seen her declining; I haven't seen her at all. Is she very ill?"

161

"Very. Probably dead by now, you understand."

Johannes looked in bewilderment at the man, at his door, wondering whether to go in or stay, at the man again, at his long coat and his hat; and he smiled the demented, painful smile of a destitute.

The old tutor continued menacingly: "Another example—is there any escaping it? *She* didn't get the one she should have had either, her childhood sweetheart—a splendid young lieutenant. He went shooting one evening, a bullet got him between the eyes and sliced his head in two. There he lay, a victim of the double-deal God had in store for him. Victoria, his bride, fell ill; a worm gnawed away at her heart till it was like a sieve; we, her friends, could see it happening. Then a few days ago she went to a party given by some people called Seier; she told me, incidentally, that you should have been there too but didn't turn up. Enough said; at this party she overtaxed her strength, memories of her beloved came rushing back, out of sheer contrariness she came to life again; she danced and danced all evening, danced like a maniac. Then she keeled over, the floor was stained scarlet where she fell; they lifted her up, carried her out and drove her home. She didn't last long."

The tutor went up to Johannes and said harshly: "Victoria is dead."

Johannes groped in front of him like a blind man.

"Dead? When did she die? Did you say Victoria is dead?"

"She is dead," answered the tutor. "She died this morning, this very morning." He put his hand in his pocket and drew out a thick letter. "And she entrusted me with this letter for you. Here it is. 'After my death,' she said. She's dead. I've given you the letter. My mission is fulfilled."

And without another word or any form of leavetaking the tutor turned on his heel, sauntered down the street, and vanished.

Johannes remained standing with the letter in his hand. Victoria was dead. Again and again he spoke her name—in a voice devoid of emotion, almost callous. He looked down at the letter and recognized the writing; there were capital letters and small letters, the lines were straight, and she who had written them was dead!

Then he made his way past the door and up the stairs, found the right key and let himself in. His room was cold and dark. He drew a chair to the window and by the last remaining light of day he read Victoria's letter.

163

Dear Johannes!

When you read this letter I shall be dead. Everything seems so strange now; I don't feel ashamed to write to you any more, and I'm writing just as if nothing had ever happened to prevent it. Before, when I was still fully alive, I would rather have suffered night and day than written to you again; but now I have started to die and I don't think in that way any longer. Strangers have seen me bleed, the doctor has examined me and says I've only got a tiny bit of one lung left, so why should I feel embarrassed any more?

I have been lying here in bed thinking about the last words I spoke to you. It was in the wood that evening. I never thought then that they would be my last words, or I would have said goodbye then and there and thanked you. Now I shall never see you again, so I'm sorry now that I didn't throw myself at your feet and kiss your shoe and the ground you trod on, to show you how far beyond words I loved you. I have been lying here yesterday and today wishing I was well enough to get away and go home again and walk in the wood and find the place where we sat when you held both my hands; because then I could lie there and see if I couldn't find some trace of you and kiss all the heather around. But now I can't come home unless perhaps I get a little bit better, as Mamma thinks I will.

Dear Johannes, it is strange to think that all I've ever managed to do was to come into the world and love you and now say goodbye to life. Imagine how strange it is to lie here and wait for the day and the hour. I am departing step by step from life and the people in the street and the rumbling of carriages; I don't suppose I shall ever see the spring again, and these houses and streets and trees in the park will still be here when I am gone. Today I managed to sit up in bed and look out the window for a little. Down by the corner I saw two people meet; they raised their hats and shook hands and laughed at what they said; but it was so strange to think that I who was lying watching them was going to die. I began thinking: those two down there don't know that I'm lying here waiting for my time; but even if they knew they would shake hands and talk to each other just the same. Last night when it was dark I thought my last hour had come, my heart stopped beating, and in the distance I seemed already to hear eternity rushing toward me. But the next moment I was back from my long journey and began breathing again. I can't begin to describe the feeling. But Mamma thinks it may only have been the river and the waterfall at home that I was hearing.

Dear God—if you only knew how much I have loved you, Johannes. I have never managed to show you, there have been so many obstacles, above all my own nature. Papa too was his own worst enemy, and I am his daughter. But now that I am about to die and it is all too late I am writing to you once again to tell you. I ask myself why I am doing so when it means little to you in any case, especially now that I am about to die; but I want so much to be near you at the end, so that at least I don't feel any lonelier than before. When you read this letter it will be as if I can see your shoulders and hands and see every movement you make as you hold the letter in front of you and read it. Then we won't be so far apart, I think to myself. I can't send for you, I haven't the right. Mamma wanted to send for you two days ago, but I'd rather write. And I'd like it best if you remembered me as I was once, before I became ill. I remember you . . . [here she had skipped a few words] . . . my eyes and eyebrows; but they are no longer the same. That is another reason I didn't want you to come. And also I want to ask you not to come and look at me in the coffin. I suppose I shall look much the same as when I was alive, only slightly paler, and I shall be in my yellow dress; but all the same, you would regret it if you came and saw me.

I've been writing this letter at intervals all day, and still I haven't managed to tell you a thousandth part of what I wanted to say. It's so terrible for me to have to die, I don't want to, I still pray to God in my heart that perhaps I may get a bit better, even if only until the spring. Then the days are light and there are leaves on the trees. If I got well again now I would never be horrid to you again, Johannes. How I've wept and thought about it! Oh God, I would go out and touch all the cobblestones and stop and thank every single step of the stairs as I passed, and be kind to everyone. It wouldn't matter how much I suffered if only I was allowed to live. I would never complain about anything again, no, I'd smile at anyone who attacked me and hit me, and thank and praise God if only I might live. My life is so unlived, I've never done anything to help anybody, and now this wasted life is going to end. If you knew how unwilling I am to die, perhaps you would do something, do everything in your power. I know you can't do much, of course; but I thought that if you and everyone else prayed for me and refused to let me go, then God would grant me life. Ah, how grateful I would be then, and I would never be unkind to anyone again, but would smile at my lot, whatever it was, if only I was allowed to live.

Mamma is sitting here weeping. She sat here all night as well and wept for me. This helps me a little, it softens the bitterness of my leaving. And today I thought: what would you do if I came up to you in the street one day in my best clothes and didn't say anything to wound you any more but gave you a rose which I had bought beforehand? But then the next moment I remembered that I can never do the things I want any more; because I know that I'm never going to get well again before I die. I weep so much, I lie still and weep ceaselessly and inconsolably; it doesn't hurt my chest except when I sob aloud. Johannes, my dear, dear friend, the only one I have loved on this earth, come to me now and be here for a little while when it begins to grow dark. I shan't weep then, but smile as well as I can, from sheer joy at your coming.

No, where are my pride and my courage! I am not my father's daughter now; but that's because my strength has left me. I have suffered for a long time now, Johannes, since long before these last days. I suffered when you were abroad, and later, ever since I came to town in the spring, I have done nothing but suffer every day. I never knew before how endlessly long the night could be. I've seen you twice in the street; once you were humming as you passed me, but you didn't see me. I'd hoped to see you at the Seiers'; but you never came. I wouldn't have spoken to you or approached you, but would have been thankful just to see you in the distance. But you never came. And then I thought that perhaps it was on my account that you never came. At eleven o'clock I began dancing, because I couldn't bear to wait any longer. Yes, Johannes, I've loved you, loved only you all my life. It's Victoria who is writing this, and God is reading it over my shoulder.

And now I must bid you farewell, it's almost dark now and I can't see any longer. Goodbye, Johannes, and thank you for every day. When I fly away from the earth I shall go on thanking you right to the end and saying your name to myself all the way. May you be happy, then, all your life, and forgive me for the wrong I've done you and for never having thrown myself at your feet and asked your forgiveness. I do so now with all my heart. Be happy, Johannes; and goodbye forever. And thank you once again for every single day and hour. I can't manage any more.

Yours,

Victoria

Now I've had the lamp lit and have got much more light. I have lain in a trance and again been far from the earth. Thank God, I didn't find it so unpleasant this time, I could even hear some music, and above all it wasn't dark. I am so thankful. But now I have no more strength left to write. Goodbye, my beloved . . .